Acknowledgements

This book is published by Enliven Press, for Didcot Writers.

The concept behind this anthology originated with two stories written by Mike Evis, each featuring the 'Half Moon Inn'. At one of Didcot Writers' regular pub socials, Alice Little suggested that for their next group anthology everyone's stories should be set at, or at least feature, a common pub. The Railway Inn is a fictional location, but named after a pub in Didcot, long-since demolished.

Didcot Writers opened international submissions for this volume in spring 2019 with a very strict brief (a version of which has been adapted for inclusion here) and the necessity for all works to go through a two-stage editing process – in order to ensure that each story could be made to refer to the same pub, and potentially also the same events and the same characters.

We would like to thank our editors Alice Little and Mike Evis for pulling the anthology together. We would also like to thank our proofreader, Rose Little.

To find out about future opportunities for publication, local writing events, workshops, competitions, and everything else we do, visit **bit.ly/didcotwriters**. You can also follow our activities on social media at **facebook.com/ didcotwriters** and follow us on Twitter at **@didcotwriters**.

A Night
at the
Railway Inn

edited by Alice Little and Mike Evis

Contents

The Railway Inn, *by Alice Little and Mike Evis*......................9

Loose Lips, *by Eugenie Pusenjak*......................15

Time for a Good Gossip, *by BJ Cutler*......................31

In Another Life, *by Margaret Gallop*......................37

Anonymous, Invisible, *by Jackie Carpenter*......................49

Back Step Chassé One, *by Tony Lawrence*......................57

More Than Meets the Eye, *by Ian Marshall*......................81

The Letter, *by Alex Fraser*......................91

Passionate Friends, *by Tracy Hewitson*......................107

An Equal Failing, *by Alice Little*......................119

Karaoke Surprise, *by Jane Andrews*......................141

Another Railway Town, *by Mike Evis*......................153

Jimmy, Eric the Panda, and Laptop John,
        by Grant Waters......................175

We'll Meet Again, *by Sheila Davie*......................191

Spirit Hunters, *by Sarah Byrne*......................197

A Portrait of a Young Woman at the Railway Inn,
        by Vanessa Waltz......................217

Ticket to Uncanny Valley, *by Rose Little*......................233

About the Authors......................249

The Railway Inn

by Alice Little and Mike Evis

The Railway Inn has stood across the road from the station ever since the railway was built. A large brick building, it has seen its share of customers, from the Victorian navvies who constructed the line, to today's commuters. Unsurprisingly, it has also seen some ups and downs.

Until the 1940s it was a peaceful pub, but during the war it saw its fair share of action, partly thanks to the barracks round the corner. It narrowly escaped destruction during a wartime bombing raid that flattened most of the buildings around it. After the war it settled back into a quieter existence as the local pub it had been before.

But changes were afoot: as the '60s and '70s wore on new estates were built swelling the local population. People moved to the town from around the UK, attracted by local industry and the proximity to London by train. The Railway Inn remained a local pub throughout, but became increasingly busy and in the 1980s it became known as the roughest pub in town: loud music, fights every night, police there all the time, a place where strangers were unwelcome.

Having survived the war, in the early 2000s the pub was not so lucky. Brought to the brink of ruin by a fraudulent landlord, the pub was left in a parlous state. This was a sad time for the Railway Inn: inattention left it tatty, the floor stained, the upholstery ripped and slashed. The brewery left it for derelict, but fortunately it was sold to a couple who saw its potential, bringing their experience of life in the big city to the town, and protecting the place when developers came to call.

With yet another change of management, today the place has turned itself around: it's amazing what several coats of paint (and a major renovation) can do. The pub still hosts a regular crowd, but also benefits from passing trade for hot breakfasts and lunchtime halves. There are always one or two older men sitting at the bar who might have been there during the old days: they've sat it all out.

But now it's a pub for all sorts of different groups: quiz night every Monday, monthly karaoke, and a weekly meeting of the local writers' group. On a Friday night the place fills up with clubbers preloading before getting the train into town. At weekends it's a pub for families – especially on a Sunday with the roast lunch on. There's a pub darts team, and the local amateur football club come in for a drink after practice. There are benches in the garden, and hanging baskets on the front of the building. There's an old piano in the corner, they say it's been there since the Second World War, it certainly sounds like it. Invariably, someone will be having a go on it.

The present owners, a young enthusiastic couple – too enthusiastic, some might say – will tell you all about the history of the pub. They claim there's a Victorian ghost: a young woman who was murdered, and there have been a couple of TV 'ghost-hunting' programmes filmed there because of it.

But they'll quickly reassure you that the pub is quite safe today, hand you the menu and recommend an artisan beer. There are chalked signs all around reminding you of their passion for running a pub and the real ale awards they've won. The inn continues to uphold its links to the railway – necessarily so: in the corner a TV screen shows the latest train times for passengers wishing to linger over their pints as long as possible before departing.

1943

Loose Lips
by Eugenie Pusenjak

Lucy Shawcross sat in the saloon bar of the Railway Inn, waiting. Through the open double doors to the public bar, she caught glimpses of khaki uniforms among the usual suits. The saloon itself was empty, save for herself, a middle-aged couple, and three elderly ladies nursing their port and lemons. Above the chatter from the public bar came the sound of piano notes, accompanied by the player's mournful, off-key tenor.

I'll find you in the morning sun; and when the night is new, I'll be looking at the moon, but I'll be seeing you…

As the grandfather clock struck eight, Lucy reapplied her lipstick. It was a new one she'd received that morning. At 8:05pm, Major Kirby entered with Peter Beresford, both shaking the rain from their overcoats. Lucy knew that Beresford was twenty-one, only two years older than herself. He had nearly completed his training at the nearby barracks and faced only one final test.

According to his file, Beresford was top of his class in code-breaking and wireless operations. A quick thinker. Adaptable. Proficient in French. Eager to serve his country. But let down by a lack of confidence. Possibly apt to talk, should he become lonely.

'…worked very hard,' Major Kirby was saying to the

younger man. 'May as well have a drink, enjoy ourselves. I can recommend the bitters.'

Now was her cue. She stood, smiling. 'Major Kirby!'

'Why – Ivy!' The Major hurried over to her table. 'Fancy seeing you here!' He kissed her cheek before turning to Beresford. 'Ivy, may I present Peter Beresford. Peter, this is Ivy Hunter. Her father and I are old friends. Roomed together at Balliol.'

'How do you do?' said Lucy, letting Beresford shake her hand. He had soft black hair, and a frank, pleasant demeanor. Just how frank, Lucy would soon find out.

'What brings you here, my dear?' asked Major Kirby.

The scripted words fell from her lips. 'I was supposed to meet an old chum who's staying with her aunt in the village. But, unfortunately, she telephoned here just ten minutes ago to say that she's indisposed. Upset stomach, possibly due to her aunt's cooking. Anyway, I had an hour before my train, so thought I may as well have a drink.'

'How fortunate for us,' replied Major Kirby. 'Look, we were about to have some supper. Why don't you join us? You could catch a later train.'

Lucy pretended to demur. 'That's very kind, but I would hate to impose.'

'You wouldn't be imposing at all,' replied Kirby. 'Do join us.'

'Yes, do, Miss Hunter,' echoed Beresford, gallantly.

'That's very kind,' Lucy said again. She followed the men to a table for three and allowed Major Kirby to order her the cod and chips, with another half of mild. Conscious of Beresford's eyes on her, she made 'conversation' with Kirby. Yes, her parents and brother were very well, thank you. Why, her father's insurance firm on Fenchurch Street was doing very nicely indeed (in reality, Mr Shawcross was a parson in East Sussex). She herself was enjoying her work as a secretary with the Ministry of Pensions. Wasn't this rain dreadful?

The meals had just arrived when the publican approached Major Kirby. 'Telephone call for you, sir.'

'Drat,' replied Kirby. 'Do excuse me.'

Now she was alone with Beresford. He grinned at her a little awkwardly. She wondered whether he'd ever had a sweetheart. She smiled back. Lucy was not vain, but she'd learned over the past six months that her blue eyes and soft curls somehow made many a chap want to confide in her. 'You aren't a bombshell, but you have a sympathetic face,' Major Kirby had said during her interview. 'I think you'll do well in this role.'

'What do you do, Mr Beresford?' she asked.

He paused. 'I suppose you could say I work with Major Kirby, for the government.'

Lucy's heart sank a little. She needed him to lie. Outrageously, if he had to. One recruit – a skinny Scotsman named Fyfe – had claimed to sell boot polish. He'd passed the test with flying colours.

'Do you mean the War Office? How interesting! What sort of work do you do there?' She hoped he would at least fudge the truth and mention one of the fictitious branches of the War Office that served as a cover for Special Ops.

'Not exactly the War Office,' Beresford replied, with a mixture of bashfulness and bravado. Lucy's heart sank a little further. He was such a sweet, earnest-looking chap. She would hate to see him lose his chance at a mission. 'You mentioned a younger brother?' he continued. 'Is he old enough to be called up yet?'

Before she could respond, Major Kirby returned, looking regretful. 'Urgent call from the office – I need to return to London right away. This war waits for no man, I'm afraid.'

Beresford stood. 'Shall I drive you?'

'No need, Peter. The next train leaves shortly. You take the car back to the barracks. And you two young ones must stay, of course. Finish your dinner. Ivy, do give my regards to your parents.'

The young man sat, looking shy, yet rather pleased at the prospect of spending some time alone in her company. The Major's ruse had worked yet again. 'I hope you don't mind, Miss Hunter?'

She threw him a warm smile. 'Not at all. You were asking me about my brother? Thomas is still at school. He's a very good football player.' She chatted lightly, watching Beresford visibly relax. 'But here I am jawing about myself, and I've barely asked you anything! You said you work with Major Kirby, but not for the War Office?'

'No. I'm with a different department.'

'How mysterious! Your work must be very important.'

'It is, rather,' said Beresford. 'Dangerous too.'

Lucy speared a piece of cod with her fork. 'Dangerous? How?'

Beresford hesitated. 'I wish I could tell you, Miss Hunter. But I'm not at liberty to say.'

The door opened, bringing a chill into the room. Lucy's stomach jolted, and the food turned to ashes in her mouth. She recognised the man who had entered. Built like a Viking god, thick-jawed, hair the colour of beaten gold: it was Egil Madsen, The Dane.

The Dane had served with the Free French in North Africa before arriving in England, and had been desperate to return to his own country to carry on the fight. Six weeks previously, Lucy had sat at this very table, listening to him sing like a puffed-up canary. He'd boasted of his prowess in explosives, boxing, and disguises. He'd showed her a couple of the latest gadgets he'd acquired at the barracks – the tiny camera in a coat button, the chocolate bar wired with a hidden charge. He'd told her how Special Ops were dropping him into Skive the following week to assist the local Danish resistance with certain acts of sabotage.

The Dane had also tried to kiss her, and she'd let him, for a while. He'd scowled when she declined his suggestion of taking one of the inn's rooms upstairs (although a small, curious, part of her was tempted for a moment – he was, after all, very handsome) and it had been with some trepidation that she walked alone across the road to the train station, listening for his footsteps.

Major Kirby had listened to her report with regret. 'A pity. Madsen would have been a strong asset for us. Still, he'll be a danger in the field if he can't keep his mouth shut.'

The next day, in London, she was ushered into the room where Egil Madsen was asked the question: 'Do you recognise this woman?' Shock, humiliation, and finally, blind fury flashed across The Dane's face. He'd spat a single word at her, one that she had never been called before. Bitch.

Now The Dane took a seat at the bar, directly in her line of sight. Lucy's heart raced, as he stared at her without expression. Why wasn't he in 'the cooler' at Inverlair in Scotland, along with the other recruits who'd proven themselves unsuited to being agents in the field? What was he doing here, at the Railway Inn?

'Miss Hunter? Are you all right?' Beresford regarded her anxiously.

She forced a smile. 'Just some fish that went down the

wrong way.' She put her knife and fork together. In the background, the piano player had struck up a new tune: 'The White Cliffs of Dover'. The three old women had finished their port and lemons, they gathered their shawls and umbrellas, and left. The middle-aged couple were standing too, the man helping the lady into her coat. Suddenly, Lucy felt very young and alone. She wished Major Kirby was still there.

'Shall I ask for a glass of water?'

Her first instinct on seeing that awful man again was to walk, run, get the blazes out. Climb through the bathroom window if necessary. Otherwise he would surely give her away, and she needed to avoid that at all costs. But... that would mean leaving the test unfinished. She had to make certain Beresford could keep his lips sealed. Also – she did some rapid mental calculations – The Dane would have left the training school before Beresford arrived. The two men had no reason to know each other. But The Dane must suspect that Beresford was a recruit. Suppose she left Beresford alone, and The Dane informed him that Lucy was an agent? The jig would be up.

Should she confront The Dane? No. If he was annoyed and caused a scene in the pub, goodness knows what he'd say. Everything – her, Major Kirby, Special Ops – could be compromised.

Only one thing for it. Lucy straightened her back. She

must buck up. Proceed with the assignment. After all, The Dane had yet not approached their table. Surely, if he wanted to expose her, he would have done so by now. Chances are he'd only come here to drink and brood.

She refocused her attention on Peter Beresford. 'I'm quite all right now, thank you. What do you enjoy doing on weekends? I love the pictures, don't you?'

'I do,' he replied, and they chatted for several minutes about their favourite films.

'There's that new one starring Greer Garson. It looks smashing.'

'Would you like to see it with me on Sunday?' asked Beresford, blushing slightly.

Lucy pulled a regretful face. 'I'd love to. But I'm busy Sunday. What about the following weekend?'

Beresford paused. 'I can't. I'm going away next Wednesday and may not be back for some time.'

'Oh?' Lucy leant forward. 'Where are you going?' She waited for his response a little breathlessly. This was the moment. Would he talk?

'France.'

Lucy sat back. The waiter collected their plates. At least Beresford waited until he'd left, before continuing. 'Mozelle, to be exact.'

'Gosh, how thrilling!' Behind Beresford, Lucy noticed The Dane order another beer. 'What will you be doing over there?' When he paused, she pressed on. 'You said your work was dangerous. You must be doing something terribly brave!'

Beresford smiled anxiously, twisting a napkin between his fingers. 'I don't feel brave. I'm awfully keen to have a go, of course. But if anything should happen to me… I'm an only child, you see. It'd be hard on my parents. As for what I'll be doing… you mustn't tell anyone.'

'I shan't.'

'I shouldn't even be telling you this. They're sending me undercover. Wireless operations. I'm to gather information from behind the lines and pass it back to London.'

Lucy suppressed a sigh. How unfortunate. He'd said just enough for her to make an unfavourable report. Such a decent-looking chap too. She patted his hand. 'I have a feeling you're going to be all right.' After all, no harm would come to Beresford in Inverlair.

'Thank you, Miss Hunter. You do have a way of cheering a fellow up.'

Lucy became aware of The Dane's eyes on her, burning into her. She had her information. Time to leave. 'My train leaves in ten minutes. Do you mind walking me over to the station?'

She and Beresford exited the pub, pulling their coats tight against the driving rain. Footsteps echoed behind them as they walked around the side of the pub to get to the main road. A glance behind revealed The Dane, following in their wake. Lucy shivered – and not from the cold. Surely The Dane wasn't going to cause her any trouble now? The road was in sight. Oh, if only they could reach it quickly!

A large hand on her shoulder spun her around, and she found herself face to face with Egil Madsen, his grey-green eyes stormy as the North Sea.

'Bitch,' he breathed.

'I say, what are you doing?' demanded Beresford.

'I've been waiting for you, Miss *Hunter*,' said The Dane, in his thick accented English. 'Or is it Miss Shawcross? Was not easy, leaving Scotland. Eyes watching all the time, yes? Lucky for me, very good at disguises.'

'Please. Leave me alone,' said Lucy, sounding braver than she felt.

Beresford frowned. 'Do you know each other?'

The Dane laughed. 'You do not know? She is a bitch, this one, a–' he uttered a word in Danish which Lucy did not understand, but instinctively knew was a profanity. 'You are from the barracks? Training school, yes? You think you happen to meet pretty girl in pub. Very friendly, interested in you. Asks lots of questions. Stroke of luck, as you English say.' His face darkened. 'But she works for *them*. Special Operations. Is testing, to see if you talk.'

'I–', Beresford blinked. 'Is this true?' His voice rose in indignation. 'You tricked me?'

Lucy's mouth was dry. 'I had to. It's my job.'

Beresford flushed with anger. 'Of all the rotten things! I suppose you think you're very clever.'

In the distance came the hiss of the locomotive, pulling into the station.

'She is a tease,' continued The Dane. 'Stops good men like us from fighting overseas. How many filthy Nazis could I have killed, if not for her?'

Icy rain trickled down the back of Lucy's collar. She wished someone would come, anyone. But the road was deserted.

'You would get *our* men killed,' she said. 'You can't keep a secret. All it takes is for one person to talk.'

The Dane stared at her for several long seconds, then turned to Beresford, grinning. 'I think we teach her a lesson, yes?' He slapped Lucy across the cheek, hard enough for it to sting. 'Your turn.'

Beresford paused, uncertain.

'Come on,' said The Dane, impatiently. He slapped Lucy again, this time over the mouth. She tasted blood.

'No,' replied Beresford. 'Take your hands off her.'

He stepped forward, but The Dane punched him, a vicious jab to the jaw which sent the younger man sprawling on the pavement. Lucy opened her mouth to scream but, incredibly, The Dane kissed her, a rough kiss, pushing his tongue deep into her mouth. He thrust her backwards against a doorway, yanked her coat open. Buttons scattered on the ground. Finally, Lucy realised The Dane's intentions. He wanted to hurt her, humiliate her, punish her.

She twisted her body, trying to get away from him, but his grip was remorseless. She heard, faintly, the whistle and accelerating chug as the train departed. The Dane reached down, fumbling at his belt. Lucy took the opportunity to slip her hand into her coat pocket. She groped through coins and handkerchiefs and a toffee before her fingers closed around what she'd been seeking.

The Dane pressed himself against her, grunting, and she raised her hand. A soft *pop!* and he fell backwards, revealing a small hole in the centre of his forehead. The smell of gunpowder filled the air for a second before being whisked away on the breeze.

At her feet, The Dane lay motionless. Rain beat down on his face against the wound, sending pink rivulets down his cheeks and into the gutter. The horror of it struck her. She had killed a man. The air seemed to spin around her and she fell to her knees, sobbing.

'Here.' Strong hands lifted her to her feet. 'Miss Hunter. Or whoever you are. You must hold it together.'

'He's...' she choked on the words. 'He's dead.'

'Yes, you shot him,' replied Beresford, holding her steady. 'But how?'

Lucy passed him the object in her trembling hand. A lipstick, concealing a 4.5mm single shot pistol. One of Special Ops' newest inventions.

Beresford inspected it, giving a low whistle. 'What will they think of next? Real question is though, what do we do with him?'

Do with him? Her lips felt numb. 'I suppose… I suppose we must call the police.'

'You could be up on a murder charge. I don't think Special Ops would get you out of something like this, or they'd be revealing to the police that they're active in this area. It's not like we have proof he was attacking you.'

The thought of it all – a trial, prison, disgrace – threatened to produce fresh sobs. Her parents. How heartbroken they'd be. 'Maybe it's what I deserve,' she said.

'Don't be silly.' Beresford sounded both older and reassuring.

'Then we must go. Leave him here. Please, Mr Beresford!'

'We can't.' Beresford spoke rapidly. She could almost see the cogs turning in his head. 'What will they do when they find the body? A Danish national. Bullet hole through the noggin. Bit of a change from their usual pickpockets and drunk and disorderlies. There'll be an investigation. They'll start asking questions. "Who else was in the pub that night?" "Did he leave with anyone?" Imagine the gossip.'

'Then what?'

Shouts of laughter came from around the block. Other patrons were leaving the Railway Inn – by the other door, thank god.

'Quick. Let's put him in the car. We'll have to drag him. Can you manage?' He lifted The Dane, staggering under the weight. 'Here, take his other arm.'

Between them, they heaved The Dane onto the back seat. His head lolled horribly. Beresford closed the door, just as a pair of drunk soldiers came around the corner. 'Getting lucky, mate?' one of them called to Beresford as they passed.

'Ignore them,' murmured Beresford. He ushered her into the car and got into the driver's seat. They pulled away from the kerb, and were soon driving away from the station.

'Where are we going?' Now that the initial shock had passed, Lucy felt her wits returning. 'Back to the barracks? Major Kirby – he could help us.'

'Isn't he in London? Ah. I see.' Beresford shot her a sharp look. 'That was all a set-up. No. What can the Major do that we can't? I say we take care of him ourselves. Save you having to answer any questions.'

He turned the car down the road which ran to the river.

*

Twenty minutes later, Lucy watched as The Dane – overcoat weighted down with rocks – sank beneath the surface.

'It was wrong of me to blab about my work, back there in the pub,' said Peter Beresford quietly, as they watched the last of the bubbles dissipate. 'I see that now. I shan't do it again, not ever. But I would like my shot at France, Miss Hunter. I think I can make a difference over there.'

'Shawcross. My name's Lucy Shawcross.'

He smiled. 'Miss Shawcross. I'd be much obliged if you were to keep mum about my… indiscretion. And I shall keep mum about yours.' He handed her back the lipstick.

They stood together silently. The rain had stopped, leaving the riverbank muddy and murky. Major Kirby would be expecting her report the following morning, what should she tell him?

On the one hand, Beresford had behaved admirably. He'd kept his head in a crisis and taken decisive action. Above all, he'd helped her when she'd needed it. Surely that counted for something? How easy it would be to omit from her report Beresford's indiscretions in the pub. On the other hand, wasn't it important to be truthful? He *had* talked. And France was such a dangerous place. She wondered whether he knew that the average life expectancy of an agent in the field was only six weeks? Such a kind boy, and nice-looking too.

Somewhere in the distance, a train whistle blew.

Time for a Good Gossip

by BJ Cutler

Two ladies made for their usual seats in the Railway Inn. They had been friends for many years, since meeting as young women in service at the big house. They had become inseparable, though they lived on opposite sides of the railway track, and now met weekly for an evening drink.

'I'll get these, the usual?' asked Nellie. 'Courtesy of my old man, not that he knows it,' she said. She hummed a little ditty to herself as she went to the bar.

Stevie made herself comfortable. She removed her woolly scarf but kept on her hat and coat, as was the custom for women in those days, and settled down for a good gossip with her friend. They only had the opportunity to meet one evening a week. The rest of the week they were busy with the usual household chores, bringing up their families – when they weren't cleaning at the big house.

'What do you mean?' asked Stevie when Nellie returned with the drinks. '"Courtesy of the old man" – I thought you said he was as tight as a fiddle?'

'Oh, I took some money out of his pocket last night; he was pissed as a newt and stinking of cheap scent. He'd been with *her* again, at the Market Tavern. So, I thought, if he could treat her, he could treat me – and I could treat you. What's good for the goose, as they say.' She laughed as she sank into her seat and took a long slow sip of her drink, the first of the evening.

The ladies listened to the pianist play 'Boogie Woogie Bugle Boy' on the out-of-tune piano.

'That tune always makes me want to dance,' said Stevie.

'I prefer "Kiss Me Goodnight, Sergeant Major",' remarked Nellie.

The ladies continued drinking and chatting. The noise in the bar became more raucous as the evening wore on. People came and went, but no one joined them in their cosy corner – although, occasionally, someone would send a drink over to them, 'for the two little old ladies over there' – that was how they were described to the barman.

The pianist played 'Knees Up Mother Brown', a few people got up and started dancing, others clapping in time to the music. Then it was back to dull chatter again as the revellers stopped for a breath and a drink from their tankards. It was always noisy in the pub, people making merry as they tried for a brief period to forget that there was a war going on.

Suddenly, Stevie said, 'How did you manage to get at his money without him seeing you?'

'I told you, he was drunk. He'd hung his wooden leg on the hook on the back of the bedroom door, followed by his trousers – there was a loud thud and leg and trousers finished up on the floor. He'd just got into bed when this happened. He said, "Oh, sod it," and within seconds he was snoring his head off. I waited a few minutes then got up and hung his leg up, and as I was hanging his trousers up… my hand accidently slipped into his trouser pocket, where I encountered a lot of loose change, your honour,' she said, bowing with a giggle. 'So I helped myself and here we are.'

'Oh, Nellie, you're a one,' Stevie said, laughing. 'I never knew he had a wooden leg. Did you make that up?'

'Not many people do know about his leg. It happened sometime during the Great War.'

'You never said that he'd been in the war.'

'He wasn't. He was a conscientious objector.'

'Really?'

'Well, sort of.' Nellie grinned. Stevie could tell she liked telling this story. 'Because he worked in the foundry he was exempt from service. He had an accident and they had to amputate his leg. Oh, don't worry, he played on it.' She was suddenly serious. 'I became his skivvy until he recovered and went back to his old haunts again.'

'How did you know he had a fancy piece?'

'The perfume. It's not the same as mine.'

'And last night? How did you know he was with her then?'

'Simple. I put on an old coat, a pair of sunglasses and a tatty headscarf, and I followed him. I sat down a few tables from them at the Market Tavern but luckily he didn't recognise me.'

'I don't know how you kept your temper. I'd have had it out with him there and then.'

'Don't worry, they didn't get away with it… at least she didn't. I… tripped. Ha! Splashed a glass of water over her, and then carried on walking as if nothing had happened.'

Both ladies dissolved in peals of laughter.

Nellie signalled to the bartender for two more drinks, only to be thwarted by the sirens signalling yet another bombing raid. They dashed, along with the others in the pub, down to the Inn's cellars. Someone produced a harmonica, and the customers spent the rest of the night singing and dancing to songs like 'In the Mood' and 'Hang out the Washing on the Siegfried Line', completely obliterating the noise of the planes until the all clear sounded.

The final song, as always, was 'We'll Meet Again'. Then, along with the others, they emerged to find the pub an island surrounded by streets of devastation.

They had had a lucky escape, and Stevie gripped Nellie's hand as they surveyed the scene.

'Best be off,' Nellie said, kissing her friend on the cheek. 'You'll be all right?'

'Chin up,' Nellie said in reply. 'See you next week.'

1952

In Another Life

by Margaret Gallop

'Same as usual, Mrs Smith?'

'Yes please, Mr Brewer.'

'I thought so. When I saw you coming up the path I thought, "There's Mrs Smith coming for her cup of Earl Grey while she waits for her granddaughter off the train." I thought, "It must be Friday again." How would you like it?'

'With milk, please, Mr Brewer, unless you have lemon?'

'Now, how would I be having lemons, Mrs Smith? I ask you. Haven't seen a lemon since before the war.'

'I live in hope, Mr Brewer.'

'So do we all, Mrs Smith, so do we all.'

Eve imagined walking through lemon groves. Half to herself she said, 'I can still remember the taste of fresh lemons. I wonder when we'll see them again. After all, the war's been over now these seven years.'

'Ours not to reason why, Mrs Smith.'

'So you say, Mr Brewer.'

'Don't torment yourself with what you're never going to get, my mother used to say,' he said.

Eve moved to the small window table from which she would be able to see her granddaughter come across the road from the station. The polished surface of the table reminded her of the sheen of a frog's back, a red-eyed frog, which she now imagined squatting before her on the table. She sat down.

Outside the window, the brick building of the railway station with its jaunty scalloped wood trim had flaking paint and was looking forlorn and dilapidated in the grey drizzle. Through the other window she could see the rubble-strewn bombsite left after the war. The pub had been lucky to survive. Now there was talk of clearing the site to make space for a car park. She pulled off her gloves and glanced away from the window at her reflection in the glass of the old grandfather clock. She straightened her felt hat, with its defiant little metal brooch which fanned out like a fighting cock's tail.

She looked around at her familiar surroundings. Her eyes strayed for comfort to the paintings either side of the clock's face: one, a sedate English pastoral scene, the other with palm trees and a tropical beach. She imagined taking off her shoes and walking along the hot sand. What fruits would those trees hold?

She knew when to look out for Kate: after the clock played 'Home Sweet Home', on the hour.

The landlord followed her gaze from his position behind the bar. 'Now, Mrs Smith, your being here reminds me to wind the clock. As you know I like things to run like clockwork round here.'

I wish he'd change his tune, Eve thought, smiling at her little joke. Was it just her impression that they had the same conversation every week? The red-eyed frog winked at her and jumped off the table into the grimy darkness below.

She looked down at her fingers. Yes, they had lost their distinctive yellow tinge, which had come from the munitions work. When the landlord's back was turned she slipped out her powder puff and patted her face using its little mirror, just in case any of that jaundiced tint still showed. Her liver had recovered, others' livers hadn't.

Collecting Kate was now the highlight of her week. Eve was no longer needed in the labour force but, while it lasted, munitions had given her a useful income with which to bring up her little daughter, Grace, her canary yellow baby. After being a 'canary girl' in the first war, she had been valued as a steadying presence in the second, to calm the flighty young girls at the factory. You needed safe, deft hands for pouring TNT into shells. She stretched her hands out and stroked their pale skin, just starting to age. An orange monarch butterfly flitted across her mind.

Mr Brewer opened the clock casement, took out a large key, and inserted it into a dark hole in the clock face. To Eve, it felt like an indignity. She was rather fond of this clock, which she felt she had known for years.

There was a call from the back of the inn.

'Oh blast,' the landlord said. 'There's the brewer's wagon come early. Excuse me, Mrs Smith.'

Glancing conspiratorially at the clock, Eve stood up and peered into the dark interior. She could see how the musical mechanism worked. The tune was played via a series of holes punched into a small metal disc, which slotted on an axel and rotated when the clock's hands reached the hour. She noticed a small box at the bottom of the case and, carefully opening it, found several other discs inside. Deftly, she unhooked 'Home Sweet Home', and hooked on another tune. Would he even notice? On contact with the mechanism, the new tune began to play; it was also an old tune, but somehow more refreshing.

I love to go a-wandering, along the mountain track.

Eve smiled to herself in the glass, and to her surprise noticed that someone else was sitting in her chair by the window. This woman wore long skirts, an unusual fashion these days. Perhaps it was the latest from Christian Dior, who was using yards of material now fabric shortages were over. And what an enormous hat! It had the brim turned up and a large fighting cock's tailfeathers against it. Something about the woman looked strangely familiar.

'Do you mind if I join you?' asked Eve, sitting in the opposite chair. 'You see, I'm looking out for someone.'

The young woman looked slightly startled, but assented. 'I'm waiting for someone myself.'

'We can watch out together.' Eve looked closer and saw how young the woman was, and then noticed there were tears in her eyes.

'Do you mind if I speak to you?' the girl asked.

'My dear, it is quite acceptable at railway stations. In fact it is almost expected.'

'You see, I have a terrible choice to make. I am meeting my boyfriend who I love very much, but I've just been given the most wonderful opportunity.'

'That's difficult,' Eve agreed, but there was something stirring in her heart.

'I've been sent a railway ticket to join a botanical expedition to the Fortunate Islands. I sent in my portfolio and got this letter, with a ticket. I've never left England before in my life, but I could be part of something big, of discoveries still to be made...'

'Then why don't you go?' Eve's stomach sank.

'Because I think my boyfriend is about to propose, and I would hate to hurt him.'

'Couldn't he wait for you?' asked Eve, sounding to her own ear more urgent than she had expected. She glanced across at their reflection in the clock glass and saw what she now most dreaded. She had been part of this tête a tête before.

There she was, Eve, herself, twenty years old, and in distress. She had never realised how beautiful she was, and there was the old woman in the felt cap urging her to take her chance and go. It was the turning point in her life. A blue African grass butterfly flew across her mind's eye, shimmering with iridescence.

Then there was a young man striding across the road towards them, his hair shining like the waves of the sea and his eyes sparkling. She felt her love for Howard rise to her throat again. Now she understood her younger self's reluctance to take up the opportunity of a lifetime, her one chance to flee grey England.

She saw, as she had remembered over and over in her head, the young Eve rising towards him and taking his hands. His bending to hear her answer. Looking at Howard, she must once and for all forgive herself for staying.

No, something was wrong. Young Eve had got out her ticket, picked up her bags and, blinking back tears, had said a hurried goodbye and darted across the road to the station. The young man looked appalled and completely shocked. This is not what happened.

Just then the grandfather clock coughed, struck the hour and sent out its tinkling tune: *I love to go a-wandering, upon the mountain track.*

What had she done? Surely not! She'd changed the course of events. The young man turned decisively and left.

Eve sat in shock.

Mr Brewer came back in, rubbing his hands. 'There's that

done for the week. Now, where was I? Ah, Miss Threadgold, I see you're in the papers again. You've won another award.'

'What's that?' said Eve. 'What do you mean?' He picked up the newspaper from the bar opened to an inner page and showed her the headlines. 'Threadgold does it again!' That was her maiden name.

Eve grabbed the paper and read, 'The research of Miss Everalla Threadgold, the renowned botanist, receives another accolade. Her decisive findings in the study of moulds have underpinned advances in medicine as well as their importance in primordial forests.'

Eve heard herself laugh and say, 'Well no one else wanted to study moulds and lichens. While they climbed trees I was looking under leaves and in the leaf litter.'

'Whatever you did, you've got another award. Is that where you're going today?'

'No,' said Eve, struggling for clarity. 'I am here to collect my…'

A death's head hawkmoth flitted across her mind. *My granddaughter*, she thought with rising panic. *Have I wiped her out? How? Just by changing the tune?*

'Hang on, Miss Threadgold, can you hear that ringing?' the landlord was saying. 'That's our new wall telephone.' He disappeared.

Eve ran to the clock and with awkward fingers quickly changed the disc back to 'Home Sweet Home'. Never had she tolerated the insipid tune so well. She looked out of the grimy window and there was her granddaughter, eyes bright, pigtails flying, running across the empty road towards her.

She stepped out and threw her arms around Kate, who welcomed the warmer than usual embrace. They walked back together arm in arm. 'Now, what would you like, Kate? Let's stay in here a minute and see if the rain stops.'

The landlord returned. 'A lemonade for my granddaughter please, Mr Brewer.'

Kate dropped her straw into the lemonade and drank happily.

'I wonder where the lemons come from for lemonade, Mr Brewer.'

'Best not to ask, Mrs Smith.' But his eyes were shining.

'There are going to be changes round here, Mrs Smith. That was the brewery on the telephone,' he said.

'Changes? I thought you preferred… er… continuity?'

'There's something in the air today, Mrs Smith.'

'Really?' said Eve cautiously. 'Not your Victorian ghost again.'

'No, far from it! We're living in Modern Times! It's 1952, you know. We're going to modernise this bar. Out with the old, in with the new, as they say. Have you heard of Formica, Mrs Smith? The latest thing!'

'Formica?'

'Wipe-clean surfaces, Mrs Smith. All this old furniture will have to go. We're going to streamline this place.'

Eve thought quickly. 'Erm… Have you any plans for the clock, Mr Brewer?'

'Quite frankly, I shall be glad to see the back of it.'

'Would you be interested in an offer?'

He looked suspicious. 'It depends what kind of offer,' he said, looking at her worn shoes.

'Five pounds?'

'It's yours.'

'I'll ask Howard to come round for it at the weekend.'

'I suppose it has an olde worlde charm, but you can't have your cake and eat it, Mrs Smith.'

'Can you not, Mr Brewer?'

1975

Anonymous, Invisible

by Jackie Carpenter

He always wanted to be anonymous. I wanted to be invisible. A subtlety maybe, but it makes all the difference. It was why he could be a bank robber and I couldn't.

All his life, he'd always wanted to hide in plain sight, to be not really seen although he was right there; for people to see him, but not really see him, not notice him. And, oh, how he'd perfected the art of looking ordinary. He didn't stand out. People thought he was unexceptional, unremarkable. He was unremarked. But inside, well now, that was a different matter. Inside, he knew how unimaginably exceptional he actually was.

He charmed me, of course. I can see that now. I know what people will say. How he took me for a fool. Or that I was – am – gullible, I didn't know what he was like.

I'm eating a sandwich at the Railway Inn, a friendly pub in a workaday town on the railway junction. The sort of place commuters stop at if they're caught out on the way to somewhere by a delay with the trains. People are always passing through, it's easy to go unnoticed.

I found this place: I'm the organiser. I always like to explore the places I visit, becoming part of the everyday life of a place, looking for a simple lunch and good coffee, observing people, wondering about their lives, not being seen. And this place was perfect, despite the mirrors all round the room – an irony I'm savouring, neither of us wanting to be seen properly, let alone over and over and from all angles.

We met when he was down on his luck, joining the flotsam and jetsam of people drifting through their days on the city streets. He heard about my group, I suppose the people who came were half laughing at and half admiring my naïve optimism that I could stand behind this disparate shifting group of homeless people and turn them into activists. It was during my first couple of years working in homelessness services, before I'd absorbed the truth that basic needs come first, and that activism was a long way out of sight for people who don't know where they'll be in a couple of hours. But people humoured me.

We don't tell many people the story, for obvious reasons. But when he did trust someone, he'd tell them how Peter had been the one person who looked out for him when he was on the streets. – 'Peter said, "You want to come to the hostel tonight. You'll get a cup of tea or coffee and biscuits. And the woman who runs it, she's something else!" – I thought, why not, I've got nothing else to do, it'll be in the warm. And I was intrigued.

'Five to seven, seven o'clock, five past seven, four of us

were sitting in the communal lounge at the hostel, elbows on the graffitied table, or sprawled on the cheap stained upholstery. We waited. Then the door burst open, banging on the wall and in she burst, all short spiky purple hair and stomping Doc Martens and eyes full of fun and passion. That was it, I was captivated!'

And I'd take over the story. 'Then you just pursued me till I gave in. Working in homelessness services, you weren't supposed to have a relationship with people who actually were homeless. But it does happen. We kept it a delicious secret for a while, and then you moved in with me, so we got away with it.' That's how we tell it.

People who meet me would be surprised to know my secret ambition is to be invisible. I'm opinionated, I can't help saying what I think. Still wearing Docs, plus vintage clothes, my style stands out. People do see me. But inside, a combination of modesty plus impostor syndrome drives my desire for invisibility.

Probably right now, he's in the bank. He'll walk in like anyone else. Stand in line like the rest, if necessary. But he always does his homework, and he's chosen a time when there'll be hardly anyone else in there. So if he's lucky he'll go straight up to the counter.

But anyway, the staff, the tellers, won't notice him. Wouldn't be alerted by any clues in his appearance or demeanour to his nefarious intent – would have nothing to tell afterwards. Would notice nothing until it was too late. Until he was right there in front of them, smiling politely but intently demanding to be taken seriously.

Of course, I don't know exactly what he says to make the point so forcefully and urgently and insistently. He never tells me what he says, how he gets the duty manager to meekly hand over the money without raising the alarm, but I already know that his people skills are his greatest asset. He knows the right thing to say at that time to that person. He's so good at reading people that he doesn't even have to think about it, he instinctively knows what to say and how to say it to get the result he's after. Not so much consciously manipulative as unconsciously shaping the world around him.

All I know is that he'll speak soft and low. Pleasantly. With a smile, just as he speaks to people in shops – building trust and rapport, as it's called in homelessness services. It's his way. He's so sure of himself, people can't even seem to think there might be an alternative way they could react to him.

Afterwards, all the staff will be able to tell the police is, 'Just looked ordinary. Average height and build, short brown hair. The sort of clothes that everyone round here wears: white T-shirt, jeans.'

Nothing to go on.

Oh, they try, the police. They set up roadblocks. Check all

the cars – in the boots and under rugs on the back seats. This isn't his first bank in the county, you see. Or even the second. So, last time, they were prepared. Determined to catch someone who'd got away with it before and made them look stupid – who they couldn't catch despite e-fit posters up everywhere.

Their big mistake was thinking, what would a bank robber do? Rather than asking, what would someone do who doesn't want to be caught? So, without a second thought, they waved the bus through the roadblock. People don't see the obvious.

There sat their bank robber, in the middle, with the stolid countryfolk, bag under the seat. Through the villages and round the houses, to the next town.

To the car and change of clothes. All also unremarkable, of course. And no one was looking for a bank robber that far away.

It worked so well that we didn't need to worry about money for quite a while. Oh, we weren't ostentatious, not daft. Didn't want to draw attention to ourselves.

It ran out in the end though, so, 'One last time,' he said.

I thought, I know he'll say that and keep saying that, but he'll always want to do it again. It's the sheer pleasure of doing it and getting away with it, as much as the money. Addictive, that high of feeling so clever.

I worked hard to persuade him that they'd catch up with

him eventually. Most people's big mistake is that they don't know when to stop. But he loves me, so he listened. And I had a plan. We agreed to meet here, at the Railway Inn, where I've been coming every afternoon for a few weeks for my coffee. Invisibility by familiarity. One last time. We won't need to do it again.

The bus should still work well, they didn't seem to have worked that bit out, or at least it was never on the news if they did. They'll be busy searching cars and outbuildings and houses for hours yet. He chose a different town this time, and will get the bus in the opposite direction. From there, he'll drive here. If they've found the car, he'll come by train. But they really don't see him at all, usually.

Me, I see him. Really see him.

With my coffee and sandwich, I sit in my corner. I'm unregarded, truly invisible. My bag is under my seat. Idly, I watch the colour TV on the shelf above the bar. I wonder if the local news will mention the bank robbery later.

I sit and wait, this one last time, waiting for him to arrive, so we can get away, off to our new life.

The door opens. I look up and, in the mirror over the bar, I see him come in, the boring clothes making him anonymous, masking the man I know and love.

1985

Back Step Chassé One

by Tony Lawrence

The smoke from the council estate chimneys mingled conspicuously with the noxious gases rising out of the coal-fired power station half a mile away. Together they infused the cold damp night air to create a pungent fog, descending slowly over our part of the Thames Valley and hanging around like an unwanted uncle at a family funeral. Street lights tinged this amorphous cloud with a yellowish, sulphurous glow, speckled by small flakes of soot drifting gently back to the ground as if to announce the start of a post-nuclear snowfall. After twenty minutes out in this weather you'd end up with a face looking like a bad case of teenage blackheads and your hair smelling like a bar of carbolic soap.

The grim winter's evening only added to my miserable mood as I pulled the Austin Maestro off the main road and into the car park of the Railway Inn. Locking the car door, we proceeded silently across the broken slabs of concrete with Cynthia holding my left arm with both her hands as if to prevent any escape.

'C'mon, yer not gettin' out of this one,' she announced as we opened the front door of the pub, deftly avoiding a copious amount of vomit pooling around the stone steps.

Ignoring the usual dregs gathered in the bar, we made our way through to the function room, the warm smoky air steaming up my glasses in the process. I could vaguely make out the sounds and shapes of people – some swirling, others standing – and then I heard the loud voice of a female booming out commands like a sergeant major on the parade ground.

'Welcome to Sylvia's Dancing and Ballroom Etiquette Class!' – here in this truly awful dump of a pub. It was the latest attempt by Landlord Billy Cummings, on the strict advice of the police, to improve the clientele of the Railway Inn or be closed down. Billy's last idea of holding a vintage motorcycle enthusiasts' rally on a Sunday afternoon had ended in a pitched battle between Hells Angels and the riot squad when drunken participants in an impromptu axe-throwing competition used a passing patrol car as their target.

I contemplated having one of my fainting episodes but, sensing my thoughts, Cynthia well and truly thwarted any exit plans by snatching the car keys from my hand and burying them in her large handbag.

'Ovver 'ere,' she said, leading me to some old wooden chairs propped against one of the walls. 'Let's get us shoes on and get started. Th'exercise'll warm us up and get us goin'. It'll be good tonight, you'll see.'

I followed silently, still peering over the top of my glasses as the mist cleared – for a second I had hoped temporary glaucoma had set in, but no chance. I took off my anorak and sat down while Cynthia reached into her bag and handed me the pair of paper-thin imitation leather dancing shoes she had given to me as a Christmas present.

Dancing shoes? That's a joke for a start, except I couldn't see anyone laughing. What the hell was I doing here anyway? Wednesday night and my home team Barnsley were playing at Reading in a mid-week third round cup-tie match and I was nowhere to be seen. It had been hard, moving down here, when all of our family and friends were still in Yorkshire, but we made it work as best we could. The promotion at Environmental Health had simply been too good to turn down and my work colleagues were a good bunch. What are they gonna say tomorrow when they discover that I, a lifelong Barnsley supporter, was not there to cheer them on and, more importantly, how do I explain that I was attending a dance class? Before I could come up with plausible excuses, Cynthia gently interrupted my thoughts.

'Brian!' she yelled. 'Stop dithering will ya. 'Urry up and get thi' shoes on.'

Heads turned in our direction and I didn't need telling twice. So I laced up my shoes with unaccustomed alacrity and stood up ready and waiting for the oncoming onslaught. A passing train caused the room to vibrate softly and the fluorescent light tubes rattled and flickered in response.

You see, Cynthia had insisted on enrolling us into dancing classes and that was that. 'I'm not 'avin' our Lizzie get one over on me again,' she'd announced to me over Christmas Eve drinks at the Labour Club. 'This time round we're gonna show 'er and 'er fancy new 'usband that we're just as good as them on a dancefloor, you'll see.'

Lizzie Shuttleworth was my sister-in-law, and still lived near Barnsley. Three years older than Cynthia, she had a history of changing husbands like our football teams changed their managers. Husband number three had appeared and swiftly exited and now husband number four was being lined up for a walk down the aisle this coming summer.

'I can't believe she's getting wed again,' I'd said to Cynthia. 'She hasn't even finished paying for her last reception yet.'

This was true. I'd had to stand as her guarantor so she could have an extended payment plan for her wedding reception in her local pub. Despite her being employed as a dispatch operative at the Littlewoods Catalogue warehouse, a job known locally as a 'packer and stacker', the landlord was not convinced as to Lizzie's financial wherewithal and credit-worthiness. So, yours truly was strong-armed to stand in when we were visiting family last Christmas, and Lizzie was allowed to put £500 down and pay off the balance at the rate of a tenner a week for two years. She still had six months to run on the tab.

'Are you sure that sailor man isn't coming back?' I'd asked. 'She must have found an address for him by now.'

'No chance,' Cynthia had replied. 'He's 'oofed it good and proper and, anyway, 'er divorce papers 'ave come through. Plus she's got the 'ots for this new fella.'

Lizzie's husband number three had been a merchant seaman from Gambia, whose rust-bucket of a ship had been unexpectedly dry-docked in Immingham for urgent repairs. This had provided the crew with some unscheduled and extended shore leave in which to enjoy the cultural delights of Humberside and beyond. Lizzie had met him at the St Leger Races meeting in Doncaster, where the packers and stackers had been enjoying their annual liquid picnic outing.

A whirlwind romance had followed leading to a hastily-arranged registry office wedding and reception before his vessel was deemed worthy to sail again. When it did, he was on it and no one had heard a word from him since. I couldn't remember his name because I couldn't pronounce it, so instead I referred to him as 'Gambino' which sounded as likely a name for a fugitive as any I could think of.

'You can't blame me really,' Lizzie said somewhat

apologetically, once her anger had subsided after around three months of Gambino's absence. 'I just fancied somethin' diff'rent from what you get round 'ere,' she explained. 'Plus, he was, er, you know, well stocked below decks if you get mi' drift,' she said lasciviously, while wiggling her index finger in the direction of her groin area. 'Part of me does miss him at times,' she added wistfully.

Well-stocked or not, Gambino was well and truly absent without leave from these parts, presumed married elsewhere. Now Lizzie was intending to marry Bernard Henry Lofthouse, Turf Accountant of Pontefract, or Bernie the Bookie as he was known locally. Twice married before and now approaching sixty-eight years old, he had form, of course, but Lizzie was undeterred. After all, he could dance, and to Lizzie that was worth a lot more than any previous indiscretions which Bernie may have committed along the way.

And this was the reason we were here on a cold and grim Wednesday evening. So that Cynthia could upstage her big sister at the summer nuptials. It's week three of a twelve-week course to learn that infernal trio of ballroom dancing, namely the jive, the tango and the cha-cha. 'Beginners Welcome' it had said in the local paper. Well, I was a beginner and I was feeling about as welcome as a turd in a swimming pool.

As a dance teacher, Sylvia Johnson had her regular class

in Oxford, but she occasionally ventured into the hinterlands on an 'outreach' basis, as if on a personal mission to convert the heathens to the religion of Ballroom and Latin. 'Reach out and I'll be there,' she could be heard bellowing on her adverts on local radio, in a badly plagiarised version of the old Four Tops soul song.

Last year, Sylvia had set up shop in the upstairs concert room of the Ravenswood Hotel, a colossal fortress-like pub in nearby Wantage. However, she had been ousted for the winter season in favour of the Faringdon Crown Green Bowling Team, who wanted the Wednesday nights to debate and discuss game theory and pre-match tactics, also known as pie and peas night.

These evenings had occasionally been enlivened by the impromptu appearance of Mavis from Milton, an ageing and un-exotic dancer-cum-stripper (stage name Véronique) who'd call in when she'd been overlooked in favour of younger models at the Hofbrauhaus. The drinkers in the downstairs snug could tell when Mavis was performing by the enthusiastic shouts of 'Put yer bloody kit back on, luv' coming from above. They'd concluded that the Crown Green Bowlers were accustomed to more refined after-dinner entertainment. Either that or they'd just simply seen it all before – probably here at the Railway, where Mavis still entertained on a regular basis.

'Come on, beginners,' yelled Sylvia. 'Let's make tracks at

the Railway,' she cackled. 'Join in and let's get dancing, there's no wallflowers allowed in here, just dancers, ha ha!' She laughed, standing in the middle of the room and looking around at her students.

A dancing star in her youth, Sylvia was, nowadays, a portrait of faded elegance, still wearing her trademark gold lamé dress and diamante shoes wherever she went. Middle-aged, middle-class, and built like a middle-weight wrestler with make-up, she feared no one. For a fleeting moment I had a picture of her standing alongside my local wrestler hero Big Daddy, both dressed in matching leotards and gold capes and ready to take on all-comers in a charity tag-team event. Then I dismissed it almost as quickly. I didn't fancy anyone's chances wrestling with Sylvia.

'Couples who dance together stay together,' she continued, 'so it's time for dancing, let's get to it now.'

The dozen or so couples already on the floor were the 'improvers' who had started half an hour earlier. The men were all dressed in polyester V-neck jumpers and their partners in matching twin sets and shoulder pads. They were supposed to assist and encourage the beginners but instead they sneered and snarled as they swirled by, reminding me of the Waltzer ride at the Whitsuntide fair which had always made me sick as a youngster.

Sylvia continued her motivation. 'Remember our saying for this year, class: let's jive in eighty-five, ha ha!'

Everyone smiled and nodded, except me. I'd be aged eighty-five before I could do this right. Sylvia walked over to the small stage which, no doubt, Mavis had often graced. A Phillips twin cassette player with built-in speakers was mounted on a chair. She opened the deck, inserted a tape into the second chamber, and pressed play. A crackling refrain of 'In the Mood' started, and Sylvia shouted out her instructions.

'Remember from last week, everyone,' she yelled. 'It's back step, chassé one, chassé two, then repeat on the other foot… ready… and a five, six, seven, eight.'

'Ouch, Brian,' cried Cynthia, 'watch mi' bloody foot, will yer?'

She was right – I had front-stepped instead of back-stepped and crushed Cynthia's right toes again. Same manoeuvre as last week. I was nothing if not consistent.

''Ow many bloody times… we start off wi' us both goin' back not for'ards,' she advised. 'Get it right, will yer!'

Sylvia had heard Cynthia's protestations and came over to assist. This was all I needed at such an early stage in proceedings. I began to pale as her considerable bulk loomed over me and pairs of eyes around the room projected their laser-like disdain towards me.

'Back step, Brian, like this,' said Sylvia, stepping nimbly on her right foot and replacing it almost instantly with her left. God, she was good. 'Then a chassé to the right and chassé to the left, and start again on the left. You can do it… now, again, off we go.'

I glanced over my right shoulder and saw the hulking figure of Big Phil and his diminutive wife Susie sidling up to us. They were also beginners, and Phil smiled and shouted some encouragement in my direction. They were neighbours of ours and had quickly become friends as they originated from the same part of the world as ourselves.

'Naw then, Bri,' he said. 'How's tha' doin' then?'

'Not very well as you can see,' I replied, 'but thanks for asking.'

'Tha'll be reet, lad, you'll get there,' said Phil. 'Just look at me, ah've bin shov'lin' in some practice since last wick.'

Phil was a striking figure of a man in more ways than one. Over six feet tall and weighing close to twenty stone, with a shaven head and short brown curly teeth, he was a mechanical shovel operator over at the power station, having been temporarily transferred down here a few years ago from his regular job at Drax near Selby. He and Susie liked the idea of waking up to the sound of birdsong instead of the morning shift siren at the colliery and so decided to settle here.

To supplement his pay, Phil was also a bouncer at Rebels, a notoriously rough and noisy heavy metal nightclub in town. In addition, he'd been a doorman here at the Railway on Sundays when another attempt to improve things had been a local bands night. Despite having such luminaries as the Merchants of Death, and Thrashed Brains on the programme, the quality of clientele had remained dismally low, and police involvement predictably higher. Perhaps if they'd merged to become 'Thrashed to Death' it may have led to some mutual improvement. Either way, when Phil was on the front door then you would be struck by his sheer physical presence – and if you were unfortunate enough to be struck by his right fist then you would earn a visit to A&E followed by a week off work.

I watched as Phil demonstrated his new-found dance skills. He lifted his left arm to reveal concentric rings of dried sweat spread across his lilac polo shirt like salt pans in the Dead Sea. His belly hung over his trousers like a badly-filled sandbag and Susie was almost bent backwards as she struggled to hold onto his outstretched hands. But his legs were chugging away like a pair of steam engine pistons, causing his considerable frame to bounce and the floor to wobble slightly under my feet.

'Very impressive, Phil,' I said, lying through my teeth. Despite his exertions, even I could see that he was at least one beat behind the music. He reminded me of Corporal Jones from *Dad's Army* standing to attention after the rest of the platoon, but this time on steroids. I wasn't going to share this observation with Big Phil though.

'Small steps, Philly dear,' shrilled Sylvia, 'and less

bouncing, more gliding. Be softer through the knees,' she intoned. 'Now, Brian,' she said, turning her attention to me. 'Chassé for me, yes, you know what a chassé is – small steps to the right, then to the left.'

I knew what a chassis was all right. It's a piece of specialist engineering genius, framing the magnificent Triumph TR7 sports car in Morgan's showroom, that I see each day walking from the train station to my office. I dream of buying this motor one day, driving through the Cotswolds with the roof down, the breeze rustling through what hair I have left, the sun beaming down as I catch a glimpse of those shapely knees and thighs emerging from the miniskirt of my gorgeous female companion on the passenger seat and wonder–

'Brian!' yelled Cynthia again. 'Concentrate on what ya doing, will ya? Sylvia's tellin' yer right and yer not list'nin',' she said sternly. 'Now, with me... no, you're out of time. Start agin. No, right foot first, and look forward, not down at yer feet. Jesus, you are useless.'

Before I could agree and seek an early bath, Sylvia intervened again. 'Get in hold first, Brian,' she said. 'That's it, good. Now, stand straight and imagine you have a balloon between you and Cynthia and you're both pressing on it gently. That's it, now hold your frame like that. Good, that's right.'

Frame. That's another thing I'm missing. My regular night

at the Mechanical Institute snooker club was on a Wednesday until this lark started up. Nothing fancy, just the comforting smell of woodbines, brown ale and microwaved Holland's meat pies, and a few frames on the green baize with my usual opponent Walter. The gentle sound of balls clicking and dropping into the pockets with the occasional congratulatory comment of 'Oh you lucky bastard' coming from a neighbouring table. It's a proper men's den, no ladies allowed, apart from Peggy behind the bar, of course, but she doesn't count.

This time last year I'd racked up my all-time highest break of forty-three. I was about to land a half century with an easy black to the top right when I was distracted by Peggy walking past the table to collect empties and lifting her blouse up to show an eager punter her latest tattoo.

'Look what you made me do now, Peg,' I'd lamented, as the black wobbled in the jaws of the pocket before gently rolling to the other end of the table.

'Hey, yer the one 'oos 'olding yer rod, not me,' she'd replied suggestively, and winked while making a jerking gesture with her cupped fist. Then she'd giggled and tottered off to the bar with the glasses. It left me wondering whether Peggy had just propositioned me and if she had, well, it's called a bloody cue and not a rod you thick–

'Brian!' cried Cynthia once more. 'Mi bloody foot again! Watch what yer doin' will yer!'

'Sorry, luv,' I said. 'I am tryin'. Let's start again.'

Apology out of the way, I attempted to soldier on, limping and skipping my way around the floor. It's week three and there's no progress in sight. I was putting a brave face on but why won't anyone just accept the simple fact that I can't bloody well dance?

The music came to an end and Sylvia walked over to the stage and rewound the cassette. 'From the top again, class,' she announced and turned to her partner. 'Patrick, my love, be a dear and go and help out Brian over there please.'

Now this was definitely not what I wanted. Patrick was all frilly red sequined shirt and tight beige trousers, with buttocks clenched so firmly he looked like he was holding a fifty pence piece between them. His head tilted thirty degrees into the air as if to avoid the smell of the peasantry around him. His bouffant silver hair bounced slightly as he walked towards us and his left glass eye stared blankly in front of him while the fleshy right one flitted around its socket like a blue-bottle trapped in an upturned jam jar.

'Just look at them tight pants, Brian,' said Phil over my shoulder. 'Tha'll know abart it if 'e gets a stiffy on, that's for cer-tin.'

If Patrick heard the comment he ignored it. 'Right then, Brian,' he said in a gentle camp voice, 'you get behind me and put your hands on my hips.'

Thank God this room didn't have all those ruddy mirrors

they had in the bar. This was excruciating enough without catching sight of how ridiculous I looked to everyone else at that moment.

He then got into hold with Cynthia and turned his head to me. 'Just follow my steps and don't forget to swivel as you move,' he said. 'All set, Cynthia? Right, here we go now. Five, six, seven, eight.'

Patrick's buttocks started to oscillate and I looked away to see that everyone was laughing at me. I was practically cuddling this oaf while trying not to inhale his revolting Hai Karate aftershave. Cynthia was on the other side of us, looking severely unimpressed.

'You can practise these steps at work, you know,' said Patrick as he continued to swivel in front of me.

Oh yes. I can just see me shimmying up the corridors at Environmental Health after typing out another improvement notice for the King Suey Chinese restaurant and take away. Will they ever stop allowing mouse droppings in their food and then telling me that they're just caraway seeds?

Just then the door opened and in walked Archie, looking a little ashen-faced. He had joined the beginners with me and Big Phil, and in all the excitement tonight I hadn't noticed he wasn't here until now. Archie is the other Yorkshireman in this town: he signed up to classes after he heard that me and Big Phil were coming along, not wanting to miss out on the chance of some social bonding, known in our parts as piss-taking.

When I say he walked in, it was actually more of a hobble. He had a walking stick in one hand and a plaster cast around his right foot, leaving his pink toes peeking out at the front.

'Sorry I'm late, Sylv,' shouted Archie. 'I 'ad an accident yesterday. Fell off mi' bloody stepladders and they've 'ad ter put this pot on mi' leg. It's not broke tho', just sprained. It'll be reet.'

You'd have thought Archie would have cut his bare toenails before venturing out tonight. Yellow, curly and opaque, they looked like deep-fried crispy wontons stuck on the end of his foot. The King Suey would have been proud to serve them with their chicken chow mein.

'Oh dear, can you walk around unassisted, Archie?' asked Sylvia. She seemed slightly concerned at the possible health and safety consequences of allowing a pot-legged old man into her dancing class.

'Course ah can,' he replied. 'And ah've driv'n 'ere mi'sen as well, so tha's no problem,' he advised. 'Ah'll still be able to do steps, Sylv, 'ah just need a partner who's weir-a-rin' Doc Martens,' he added with a chortle. He noticed me still holding onto Patrick's hips and said, 'How do, Brian, got thi sen a new mate then?'

At last, someone who was at my level. Archie Schofield

was known to everyone here. A self-employed painter and decorator since I was in short pants, he still followed his trade despite being well into his seventies. He'd moved down here over twenty years ago after his daughter met and married a railwayman, and his own wife left him following an extended affair with a driving instructor. He would often greet you in the street with a cheery, ''Ow do, ah'll be round at yours next wick or wick after,' even though you'd not asked him to do any work at your house.

Archie's doctor had advised him to keep active in his elderly years and to do something each day that left him slightly out of breath. So he'd started smoking and took to reading girlie mags during his lunch breaks. 'Just 'ave a look at these beauties,' he would say to bewildered pensioners who were expecting to see a picture of the latest quick-drying and washable emulsions. 'Thar's not much fat on yon big lass naw, is tha?'

Archie was nothing if not an optimist and he'd battled adversity all his working life. For starters he was colour-blind, which was not a good quality to have in the painting business. This led to countless re-visits to disgruntled customers who simply wanted all four walls in their living room to match each other. Also, he was incapable of hanging wallpaper in a straight line, perpendicular to the floor and ceiling, instead always leaving it listing about five degrees to the left.

'It's wi'all this sub-sistence from railway wagons over years, you see,' he'd explain when challenged about this apparent failing in his workmanship. 'It meks the walls go wonky. But not ta worry, ah'll put a matching dildo rail in top and bottom and tha' won't notice any diff'rence really.' Archie and his dado rails could be found in people's houses all over, and wherever subsidence had occurred.

'Patrick, partner up with Archie next to Philly and Susie, would you, dear,' said Sylvia, attempting to corral the six of us into one corner of the hall. I sensed that she intended on making a small 'losers loop' for us to go around so as to not offend the improvers.

Patrick's good eye did a quick scan of Archie's pot leg and, not wishing to risk a broken foot, he leant forward from his ankles and, raising his hands, he announced with a smile, 'I'll be your lady this evening, Archie.'

'Fine wi' me, Patricia,' responded Archie. Mindful of Patrick's trouser department, he also leant forward from his ankles to meet Patrick's hands. They went into hold looking like two sides of an A-frame tent. An Alsatian dog could have passed unnoticed along the gap between their opposing feet.

'Right then, class, off we go again,' shouted Sylvia. 'Improvers, you're looking brilliant. Beginners get ready for the music.'

Once again, 'In the mood' started up (*doesn't she have any other bloody tunes on this cassette?* I wondered) and Sylvia counted us in, 'Five, six seven eight.' Off we went with a back step, then it's THUMP-EE-THUMP, THUMP-EE-THUMP! I looked up as Archie's plastered right foot stomped on the floor with enough force to leave small indentations in the polished laminate, and little piles of white dust began to form around his feet.

'Stop, stop,' yelled Sylvia. 'Archie, dear, that's way, way too heavy. You're damaging the floor with your pot leg. Be gentle, much softer and smoother please,' she pleaded. 'And Philly, dear, let Susie's balls touch the floor.'

'Eh?' replied Phil, and I too was perplexed by this strange request.

'The balls of her feet, dear,' Sylvia explained. 'The poor lass is on her tiptoes because you're lifting her way too high.'

Phil looked at his wife and nodded. Acknowledging his error he dropped his arms by six inches and Susie came back down to floor level with a sigh of relief.

Sylvia turned her attention to Archie again, who was trying to sweep up the plaster grains with his left foot while still holding onto Patrick. 'Not ta worry, Sylv,' he said, 'ah'll just nip ah't and fetch a dust-sheet from van.' Letting go of Patrick, he hobbled towards the door, lighting up a Park Drive to help catch his breath.

Sylvia continued with her advice, this time in my

direction. 'Brian, dear,' she said, 'concentrate on what you are doing. Cynthia's doing really well and you're not keeping up with her. Come on now, you can do it.'

I looked back at Sylvia and saw that the first signs of exasperation were sweeping across her face. Maybe she'd realised even she could only outreach so far. Week three and this is all we have to show for progress. That wouldn't go down well in the radio adverts.

The improvers were twirling past us sending out silent looks of contempt at this car crash taking place on their highway of dance. Their haughty looks said it all, and in that moment a blinding flash of reality hit me: I realised there was nothing in this unequal world of ours that divided the classes more than the ability to dance. Forget the three bed semi-detached with adjoining car-port: ballroom dancing was the one true path to upward mobility and higher social equality.

Those economic revolutionaries at the Council had got it all back to front in their zest for a new world order. Handing out rent rebates and cheap bus fares was all well and good for getting the workers out of bed and off to the factories in the morning, but they were just gimmicks really.

'What if they'd introduced compulsory dance classes for all the primary school kids twenty-five years ago?' I said absent-mindedly to Cynthia.

She looked up at me and replied, 'Well, in that case yer

might 'ave just reached improver stage by now.'

Yes, we'd all be the same, I thought, proper dancers, every one of us, and any conflicts would be resolved in a Mecca ballroom.

But now it's too late. The Council will be disbanded shortly on Government orders and Cha-cha Guevera is not a resident of these parts, nor is he ever likely to be. The promised social revolution hasn't happened. I mean, just look at us here: we're going round the floor in an anticlockwise motion when the rest of the world turns clockwise. It's not right to go against the natural order of things.

I glanced at Cynthia, and then around at my fellow beginners in the arms of their loved ones – Patrick excluded of course – and wondered if we really were in our natural surroundings here. Let's face it, we were all fighting a losing battle and maybe it was time to come to our senses and quit. Dancing wasn't for us. A couple of pints at the more serene Market Tavern would be far more satisfying, even if I had to fork out and buy the first round.

Just as I was about to suggest this course of action, Cynthia sensed my thoughts and fixed me with her sternest steely look. She meant business, that's for sure. 'Brian, we're dancin' and tha's all there is to it,' she lectured. 'So get yer arse in gear and buck yer ideas up, pronto. We're dancin', end of.'

'That's it, Cynthia, you tell him, girl,' enjoined Sylvia, rejuvenated at this rallying call in the ranks. 'Remember that every dance journey starts with a single back-step,' she announced, badly paraphrasing Lao Tzu, the ancient Chinese philosopher. He sounded like another bloody revolutionary in my book.

Just then we heard shouts and yells as Archie tripped over the dust sheet he'd been carrying and tumbled to the ground. I sighed in quiet resignation and grimaced. Getting back into hold with Cynthia I realised one other philosophical truth: it's only week three and it's going to be a long journey to the summer wedding.

2007

More Than Meets the Eye

by Ian Marshall

A will sat among a plethora of legal documents on the mahogany desk. An antique wooden lampstand, with 'The Ravenswood Hotel' carved into it vertically, perched precariously on the corner: it was too nice to have downstairs with all the punters. The low-wattage bulb emitted a soft light. Sitting at the desk with a glass of merlot, Joshua sucked a thoughtful tooth while staring down into the road from the office window. He pulled some chest hair through a hole between his shirt buttons and twizzled it aimlessly before reverting to tugging at his trendy stubble.

'Josh-wa', 'Josh-you-are', 'Joshee'. He played around with his name. It amused him, even though it wasn't new anymore. It wasn't his real name, but he'd grown into it these past few years. And now he was about to move on: he'd be given a new name, a new story, a new identity. He sat back and reflected on his time at the pub.

'Hello, it's Joshua Moon, from the Railway Inn,' he said to himself, as if making a call to a supplier. He recalled how, when he was first told he'd be coming here, he looked up the 1861 census online, found the pub and saw the name Joshua Moon, living there with his wife and nine little

Moons. You couldn't raise a family of that size here now, he reflected. It's too busy.

Was it foolish to have adopted the same name as a previous landlord? Probably, but no one had done the same research, so it wasn't something he'd had to address. And Joshua Moon was a better name than Bertie Brewer, who had been landlord in the 1950s. It seemed too good to be true, a publican called Brewer: what were the chances he wasn't what he seemed either? Joshua was a much nicer name, but his wife could hardly copy the old landlady's name. 'Philadelphia' was a Christian name whose era had long since gone. No, Nicola was a sound English name. They had worked assiduously to conceal every conceivable trace of their native eastern European accents and had developed generic Home Counties voices. They fitted in perfectly.

He glanced down at the railway tracks and shuddered at the thought of the demise of his predecessor at the Railway Inn. Then he wondered which previous landlord it was who had put all those blasted mirrors up in the bar. He couldn't understand why anyone would do that, it was like being watched all the time. The first thing Joshua had done was to have them all taken down. His eyes meandered across the beer garden, fully illuminated by lights which attracted the local moth community.

Down the road to the left of the pub he watched a tall

muscular man, slightly thinning on top, as he carried a sleeping girl over his shoulder. Wearing a pink party dress covered in sequins, she appeared dead to the world. The dad slowly unlocked the front door to their house, desperately trying not to make a noise. Joshua wondered whether she was really asleep or just pretending, to avoid having to wash before bedtime, just like he used to do when he was little, and his father would carry him up the stairs and put him to bed still in his clothes.

He waited until the dad quietly closed the door before attempting to shred another document. A message lit up on the bin: it was full, and the machine would refuse to co-operate until he emptied it. He sighed but didn't move. It had been a long evening, going through the paperwork, destroying the evidence.

He could hear voices downstairs in the pub, belonging to members of the writers' group. Their meeting must have finished. Good. They really were a pain, always complaining: the pub was too hot, too cold or too noisy, and yet they were almost always the last people to leave. If they didn't like it, why did they stay there so long? He'd begun to take Wednesday evenings off just to avoid them, coming upstairs to the office instead to do his paperwork, which these days was mainly about covering his tracks. Those writers pushed him to the limit. It was as much as he could do to smile and say he would try to fix things for them. One day soon, he felt sure, he would tell them where to stick their writing. He sipped his merlot and tried to calm down.

The writers wound him up, but playing with the Sunday morning football team always relaxed him. They played on the rec down the road, then came back to the inn for a drink. He was acutely aware that his footballing education fell short of his teammates', and that it showed in the way he played. But football was a release from his work – whether running the pub or working for his government – and they all did their best and pulled together. He was proud of that team.

His mind wandered to the football games of his youth. How he had enjoyed standing on the cold terraces at Spartak, cheering the players on. The White Angels had been his team, a beacon of light in his childhood. He grinned as he savoured these far off memories: the moments of collective joy at the end of a close match after the referee had blown the final whistle, followed by the long trek home through dimly lit streets. Happy days.

Then, too soon, his dad was taken by a brain aneurysm, and he'd left to go to university, and while there had been recruited, ending up in England. Would he ever go back home? Possibly, but not yet. It wasn't on the horizon.

But there were changes afoot. There had been contact from his paymasters and he knew his time at the pub would be ending soon. He'd received instructions to put it on the market next month, and his cover story was in place. He would be sorry to leave, but a promotion was not to be sniffed at. Assuming that was what was coming his way. After all, he and his wife had done an excellent job, even if he said so himself: profits had been made, dividends issued and money *smurfed*. He loved that word, he learnt it in his training: a colloquialism for money laundering.

They had studied so hard learning informal expressions. And adjectives! Oh, my goodness! He recalled the months spent on the correct order of adjectives in English sentences, so as not to betray his foreign background.

'Orderliness is instinctive,' his tutor used to say. 'Natural English speakers know the correct sequence of words and phrases. They can spot a fraud a mile off.'

'I think I've passed that test,' he mused.

Yes, they had done well at the pub, and had covered their tracks effectively. There was nothing left that led back to their employers, except maybe some of these documents waiting to be shredded. The pub accounts had recently been audited and signed off by a large UK accountancy firm. The junior auditors were so wet behind the ears they hadn't suspected a thing. As for the partner in charge, he must have thought he was making easy money on such a small job. He was right, of course, but that was why his firm was chosen. VAT, PAYE and corporation tax payments were all up to date. The business was squeaky clean, whiter than white, just the way it should be.

He lifted his glass once more. 'Cheers,' he said to himself. 'A job well done.' Then he chastised himself for getting smug too soon. 'Idiot!'

It would be sad to leave the Railway Inn. The pub had been good to them. But he and his wife would quickly become just another entry in the long line of the pub's owners and managers stretching back over a century and a half. Would some historian in the future find it funny that there had been two Joshua Moons at the Railway Inn? He'd be long gone by then.

He'd also be sad to leave the guys on the football team. Sunday mornings had been the highlight of his week.

Yes, there had been some good times here. He glanced at the signed photo of that ghost-hunting woman off the telly. It had been taken after two days of filming at the pub. People were always coming round looking for the ghost that was supposed to be there, so it was hardly surprising the TV people had come round in the end. It had been a bit of an odd experience, but the episode had been all right. They'd had a good night round the telly in the bar, watching it all together. Joshua considered them all to be money-grabbing charlatans – but if they wanted to film a follow up programme, he wouldn't be averse to the free publicity. Even now, new customers mentioned that show. He smiled at his own hypocrisy. He could have been a ghost detective or whatever they called themselves. He'd fit in perfectly with them, he reckoned: searching in shadows for people who didn't want to be found, never letting on what he really thought, taking money from idiots who believe the world to be different to what it really was.

After sitting motionless for long enough to pass as a Madam Tussauds exhibit, he thought he should stop daydreaming and get on with the shredding. But he hadn't emptied the bin yet. 'It can wait,' he thought, 'it's late.' The stragglers had long since left the pub. He could hear the staff putting used glasses into the washer. Nicola would be cashing up. He couldn't be bothered to do any more tonight.

He picked up his wine glass and took a slug of the red stuff. He half closed his eyes and swirled the liquid around his mouth. He made the requisite slurping noises, like a wine-tasting expert, while nodding his head sagely. He commentated in his head: 'There are strawberries, with a delightful a hint of blackcurrant and the bouquet of vanilla is exquisite.' Whatever. Finally, he swallowed. The house red had never undergone such a rigorous examination.

He picked up a small blue pen borrowed from Argos, and was about to write down some profound thoughts about the vintage, but instead drew a series of ellipses, the rings of Saturn without the planet itself. He liked the shape and added some triangles at random intervals around the disc.

He was oblivious to the outside world. He stopped, contemplated, selected a yellow felt tip from his desk tidy, the cheapest WH Smith had to offer, and coloured in some of the shapes. This process was in full swing when a voice resonated from downstairs. It was Nicola.

'The police are here, darling. They'd like a word.'

His unfocused gaze snapped back to reality. He bundled up the will with the other documents on his desk and hid them in the desk drawer, cursing the 'bin full' message still blinking on the shredder. He locked the drawer and called out, 'OK. Thanks, love. I'll be right down.'

2011

The Letter

by Alex Fraser

David carefully folded the letter, put it back in its expensive bonded envelope and pushed it deep into the pocket of his overalls. The cracked overflow in the ladies' toilet would have to wait. There were decisions to be made and if David had learnt anything from fifteen years at the investment bank it was that decisions had to be made quickly. But first, he would have to speak with Judith.

'David, it's nearly ten and the organic veg hasn't arrived yet from Pearsons, can you get onto them, and the fishmonger as well? They're hopeless, they let us down last week and Konrad says there'll be no specials for lunch unless they arrive soon.'

After twelve years of marriage, David knew that panicky tone of Judith's could easily spill over into a full-on shouting match unless he complied. When it came to organisation of suppliers or staff or anything to do with the day-to-day running of the pub, Judith was at the top of the Premier League.

'And have you fixed the overflow? Ruth said there was water all over the floor last evening, she made quite a thing about it. Oh, and Shane's girlfriend called, he's been up all night with D and V apparently and won't be in, you'll have to cover the lunchtime bar.'

David did not enjoy doing the lunchtime bar. The regulars were a bunch of dystopian retirees, never happier than when moaning about 'the state of the nation', 'the youth of today' or 'the number of Poles/Romanians/general undesirables'. On and on they went, the spittle from their jowly mouths spraying over the newly fitted solid oak bar as they spat out their invective against the modern world. David had once made the mistake of pointing out who cleaned the toilets they used, cooked the food they ate, and drove them home when they could no longer stand, but they either couldn't or wouldn't understand.

But right now David's mind was on more important matters than having to endure the wittering of the lunchtime bores. He'd have to tell Judith what was in the letter – but before the meeting or afterwards? He was sure she'd love the idea, but even after all this time together he sometimes couldn't second guess his wife's reaction. When he suggested buying the pub, two years ago, he thought she'd never be interested – but she had reacted positively, maybe recognising her modelling days were behind her and that it was time for them both to find a new challenge. And in truth it was Judith's extrovert can-do nature that was the driving force behind their success. David still called the financial shots, however.

Thankfully, Friday lunchtimes were usually quiet. The old bores were fewer in number, probably taking their bile to the local golf club where the drinks were cheaper – as David was regularly reminded. Later that afternoon the Paddington train would disgorge the early risers as they made their return to the Oxfordshire countryside in good time for the weekend before the commuting whirligig tore them away again on Monday morning.

'A swift half, Roger?' said one punter to his neighbour at the bar as he sat down.

'No thanks, Bill, I've already had mine. I've got to head back to the vicarage and write my sermon for Sunday before tonight's meeting.'

So Bill had a pint by himself, perched in the corner behind the pool table, where the light from the window allowed him to better focus his rheumy eyes on the Times crossword. He had another, and one more with a whisky chaser, before finally throwing his pen down with a flourish.

Pulling on his tweed jacket and adjusting his Panama hat in the mirror by the door he mumbled thanks to David. 'See you at the meeting tonight, I've prepared a short declamation.'

David instinctively felt for the envelope in his pocket and smiled.

'Bastards, those developers,' Bill muttered as he opened

the door and left.

*

The Railway Inn had a long history, dating back to when it was built as a drinking den for the navvies who constructed Brunel's Great Western Railway, when the town was little more than a halt between Reading and Swindon. It had survived the War, but was almost finished off in the 2000s when it was closed for long months for some kind of police investigation – MI5, some of the locals said. David didn't know about that, but he knew that it had almost been curtains for the Railway Inn, as commuters arriving off the 5:45 found other haunts.

When the Railway Inn finally did reopen, it quickly became the runt of the brewery's litter, unloved, unwanted and in need of putting out of its misery. By 2008 they realised that the Inn was better off their books. It became one of a 'managed portfolio of prime location properties' which could 'benefit from improvement' by new owners prepared to 'inject energy and commitment' – and about half a million quid. After languishing for years like a rotting hulk on a beach, the freehold was eventually sold.

When David and Judith first came to the Railway, commuters still shunned it, and most locals hurried past. The garden, if there had ever been one, was a dumping ground for defunct fridges, rusting ovens and discarded food containers. Inside, the cheap plywood benches had detached from the wall and the maroon covers had split open with smoke stained yellow foam emerging like magma from a long-extinct volcano. Food debris, which would have needed carbon dating to determine how long it had lain there, littered the torn and creased linoleum, sticky with years of grease and spilt beer. Anyone brave enough to enter the frosted glass door and step over the surely ironic 'Welcome' rushmat would have to endure dead-eyed stares and barely concealed aggression from the few lowlife patrons who drank there. The Railway Inn had all the intimidating atmosphere of a Siberian gulag but it was not as warm.

David had dreamt for years of moving out of London. The daily commute from Kent to Finsbury Circus wore him down. The 6am starts for the benefit of the Far East markets, the tedium of being stranded in front of a computer screen for the next twelve or more hours and the stress when the numbers went red had become too much to bear. Burnt out in his mid-thirties, already diagnosed with a peptic ulcer, he knew he had to change his lifestyle.

Judith's assignments were falling away now that she was no longer a willowy twenty-one year-old, and she had a designer's eye for the zeitgeist. To David's surprise, she was prepared to give up London life and follow his dream. Of course, they would miss the income – let's face it, why would anyone do his job apart from for the money – but when the next bonus hit his account they had enough to pay cash for a new project, and they had faith that his business acumen and her cool taste could salvage a rotting hulk and transform it into a luxury cruiser.

*

'How many are we expecting for the meeting tonight?' asked Judith. They were in the spruce panelled office above the bar.

'I don't know, thirty, maybe forty. There's been a lot of local interest,' said David.

'We'll have to use the function room, you'll need to set the chairs out.'

'Judy, there's something I need to talk to you about and it's–'

'Not now, David, I need to run through the evening menus with Konrad and we've run out of lemons so I'll have to go to Waitrose. The Chablis needs putting in the fridge and the craft beers have to go in the cellar.'

'All right, I get it, but let me read this to you,' David said as he fished out the envelope from his pocket. But Judith had already gone.

*

'The planning application was submitted last week but only registered with the council on Wednesday, hence the delay in notifying concerned residents. Let me read to you the description of what is proposed…'

Bill King loved an audience, Judith thought. Thirty years as a classics teacher at one of the country's most prestigious public schools had given him an air of effortless superiority. He was seemingly unaware that he was not addressing a group of tousled-haired future leaders of the country.

'…a development of up to six hundred two, three and four bedroomed residential units of which at least thirty percent shall be for affordable rent.' He paused for effect, looking over his half-moon glasses for signs of opprobrium from the throng of concerned local residents in front of him. '…together with play areas, landscaping and formation of a new access from Wallington Road on land adjoining the Railway Inn.'

Judith was sitting in the front row. Well into his stride now, Bill continued, 'You will be gratified to learn that when I spoke with the planning officer she indicated that the application would probably be refused–' a loud cheer went up '–but that the planning committee would be making the decision and, should they refuse permission, the developers will almost certainly appeal.' Loud moans and catcalls greeted this bad news.

'So, ladies and gentlemen, we have a fight on our hands. I hardly need add that such a development would entirely destroy the verdant beauty of this part of our beloved town, and change its character beyond recognition. It is our right, no, indeed, our duty to use all of the powers we have to avoid this abominable outrage intended to be foisted on our town. The Greeks gave us democracy – literally rule by the people – and our democratic engagement will defeat those determined to subjugate us. In the words of Cicero, *salus populi suprema lex esti*, which, for the uninitiated –' Bill peered over his spectacles again searching in vain for signs of intelligent life, '– I will construe: let the welfare of the people be the ultimate law.'

Bill had certainly dressed for the occasion: a maroon bow tie and matching handkerchief dangling from the breast pocket of the same tweed jacket he had worn earlier, the elbows covered with worn leather patches. There was probably still chalk dust in his pockets, thought Judith absently as he rambled on.

A voice called out from the back of the room. Judith turned and was amazed to see thirty or so people standing at the back in addition to all the chairs David had put out earlier being filled with attentive listeners. Clearly he had underestimated the strength of the hostility of the middle classes to a housing development that might adversely affect their house prices. I must have a word with David afterwards, thought Judith.

'Excuse me, can I just ask…' said a voice.

Bill looked up sharply. He was not used to being interrupted. 'I'll take questions at the end, thank you. Now, as I was saying….' Bill droned on for several more minutes.

The hoi polloi were getting restless.

When Bill next paused for breath, Judith rose from her seat and faced the audience. The room was hot and sweaty.

'Bill has very ably and with great erudition as always–' there were some ironic sniggers from some at the back '–set out the position, so I suggest we break for fifteen minutes for some refreshment, and then come back and decide what we as a community are going to do about this assault on our town.'

Some sporadic clapping broke out and there were murmurs of assent as the assembled throng moved towards the door and back into the bar.

'Has anyone seen David anywhere?' asked Judith.

*

David was upstairs in the office, waiting for Judith.

'What are you doing here?' she asked. 'Why weren't you listening to the talk? There's so much opposition to this development.'

'Take a look at this.'

David passed her the letter that he had been hanging onto since the morning. Judith looked at the headed notepaper: 'Seventh Heaven Estates – your vision is our mission.'

'Read it,' urged David.

'Dear Mr and Mrs Worth,' she read. 'You may be aware that through our agents we have recently lodged an outline planning application with the local council for up to six hundred houses on the land adjoining the Railway Inn. We have been advised that due to government policies to meet housing development targets our application would stand an excellent chance of success were our plans to include the building and curtilage of the Railway Inn of which we understand you are the freehold owners. Therefore, we are proposing, subject to contract, to offer the sum of £1.5m for the acquisition of your property conditional on planning permission being granted. We would be more than happy to discuss any questions you may have. We look forward to hearing from you.'

Judith's hands were shaking as she handed the letter back to David. He noticed she had gone pale and her words came in deep heavy breaths.

'My God, I don't believe it, they want to buy the pub and then knock it down to build more houses.'

'They're offering us nearly five times what we paid for it. Even allowing for the work we've carried out we'd be nearly a million better off! And that's just their opening offer; think what they would go to once we get solicitors involved, you know what a Rottweiler Tom is.'

Judith looked towards the door down to the bar. In David's excitement he might be overheard.

'Just think what we could do with that,' he was saying. 'We could buy a project down in Cornwall and make it even more successful than this place! Isn't it incredible?' David gripped Judith hard by the arm. 'This is a miracle, it gives us all we want.'

Judith's whole body was now shaking. David looked at her, her liquid blue eyes were moistened with tears.

Just then there was a loud rap on the door. 'We're going back in,' a voice said.

'I must get back,' Judith said.

'You'll have to play along with them for the time being, don't say a word, they won't exactly be over the moon about it.'

Judith went back downstairs to the meeting. Alone in the office, David punched the air. What a turn up it was! He returned to his iPad and brought up the properties he'd been looking at most of the afternoon. Yes, there'd be a backlash from the locals, but what the hell, they'd be gone as soon as contracts had been exchanged and it would be one in the eye for those tedious lunchtime bastards, they'd have to find some other mug to bore to death.

Think of it, a life by the sea. I could buy a boat, thought David, and go out fishing, bringing in the catch for that evening's menu. The Railway Inn had been a good first project for them, they had turned it around and put their hearts and souls into it – especially Judith, of course – but here was a chance to really go big. They could hire a top chef; the West Country was the place to be, no doubt about it. It would be hard to leave, but these opportunities don't come around every day. Judith would love it, the chance for another place to develop from scratch, the challenge of getting into all the best gastro pub guides. She'd said she wanted to offer rooms too, and had started redecorating upstairs, but he hadn't wanted to allocate much money to it when the turnover would be so small: now they could afford to do things properly at a new place.

David wanted to see how Judith was getting on in the function room. She was doing the right thing, carrying on as normal, making sure everyone was happy – well, as happy as they could be with a six hundred-plus development about to destroy the town. David smiled broadly. She's better at this sort of stuff than me. They'll all be wondering why I'm looking so happy. I must contain it, David warned himself.

He went down into the bar area. There was a couple sitting by the window looking at the menu, but otherwise it was unusually deserted for a Friday evening. It seemed that half the town was in the function room, desperate to put a stop to Seventh Heaven's plans. He opened the door, having to push against someone blocking the entrance, and looked in. It was packed. Several regulars met his eye and grimly smiled a greeting to him. The combination of heat and the smell of sweat was almost overpowering. David saw Judith at the front addressing the throng.

'...and we'll take the fight to these developers with all of our strength and will. We'll set up a fighting fund, have a petition at the bar, we'll employ planning consultants, lawyers, PR people, get our local councillors onside, we will not let our town be destroyed by these greedy developers who are only interested in their own profits.'

Despite the warmth of the room David felt a cold sweat break out. His mouth was dry and he felt his tongue sticking to the roof of his mouth. He wanted to call out to her but he found himself paralysed. He tried to catch Judith's eye, she must have seen him come in at the back. Judith's words were now being drowned out by applause, yells and whoops of support.

Judith continued once she could make herself heard again. 'The Railway Inn will be at the heart of this opposition and,' she said, looking directly towards David for the first time, 'David and I are going to lead the fight.' The eyes of the whole room turned and looked towards him.

'Aren't we, David?'

2012

Passionate Friends

by Tracy Hewitson

'How about, "Marriage, ultimately, is the practice of becoming passionate friends" – Harville Hendrix?' Jane mentally marked the quote for the wedding card but carried on scrolling.

'Who's Harville Hendrix? Oh, wait a minute I suppose he's one of your self-help gurus,' her husband Jo snorted from the driver's seat.

Jane shifted and gazed out the car window. 'Well, as it happens, yes, he's an American author–' and was going to talk about his book *Getting the Love You Want* but was cut off by Jo's sniggering.

'OK, why don't you just focus on the driving so that we actually get to this pub? Then I can write the card and get ready.'

'As you wish, my love,' Jo replied unconvincingly, and slightly increased the pressure on the accelerator.

Jane turned her face again to the passing view of the countryside and began to anticipate the day ahead. Gerry and Sam had chosen a really quaint village church for the service, and the reception was to be held in the church hall only a few yards away. It was a four o'clock start and then straight on to the reception.

The website for the church was where Jo had found the details of the Railway Inn; it had only just started offering rooms, so the rates were very reasonable. The photos on TripAdvisor looked OK. The rooms seemed cosy enough, and the bar looked respectable. The frontage was embellished with burgeoning flower baskets and welcoming signboards. Most of the family were staying in a swanky hotel nearer the church, and it turned out that Jane and Jo were the only wedding guests at the pub. They could have got there by train, but what with all the paraphernalia they had to take with them it was a better option to drive, and trust that the car didn't come to any harm in the pub car park.

On the whole though it wasn't the pub that was uppermost in Jane's mind. Ever since Gerry had announced her engagement to her long-term boyfriend Sam a year ago, Jane had been dwelling more and more often on the past – on that time, ten years ago now, when they were all friends at uni: Jane, Jo, Gerry, Mark, Sally and Sarah. The old gang had been talking a lot in the run up to the wedding, and it felt like only yesterday that they were together. They had been very close. It was only Sarah no one had heard from for years. At graduation she had told the others that she planned on moving up to Scotland to do some research for a masters degree. Gerry had sent a wedding invitation to

Sarah's sister's address and asked that it be passed on. It was the best she could do.

Of course, things had been different for Jane with Jo. They had paired up half way through the final year, so were not just friends anymore. It changed the dynamic of the group to some extent, but even more so when they began to build a life after uni. So, Jane looked forward to seeing everyone together again, her excitement outweighing the slight twinge of melancholy she felt, missing those days.

Jane was snapped out of her daydreaming when Jo turned in at the Railway Inn, pulling up beside a low brick wall. Jane looked up at the building and smiled. The sight of the flowers adorning the pub and garden instantly raised her spirits in anticipation of the wedding flowers. Any melancholy disappeared in a puff of pollen.

'It looks lovely,' Jane said, looking at Jo for confirmation.

'I'm looking forward to a pint before the taxi comes.' Jo grimaced as he dragged the suitcase out of the car.

They found the manager behind the bar and, while waiting for him to finish serving, took a look around. Jane saw Jo looking at the television and knew what he was thinking: that he'd much rather stay in the bar all afternoon and watch the football. Jane could read his mind.

Up in their room, the décor was a pleasing mix of rustic charm and contemporary design. Jane and Jo were soon unpacked, showered and changed, and standing at the bar in all their finery. Two pints and two gin and tonics later, they got into the taxi to head to the church.

*

It was gone midnight when they returned. They climbed out of the taxi at the back of the pub, and Jo staggered through the garden to the residents' entrance. Jane hung back, still in control of herself. The day had been blessed with good weather and it looked like the Railway Inn had benefited from hosting many customers – too many to clear up after. The air was heavy with the sour smell of spilt beer and cigarettes. Jo walked up the shallow ramp and put the key in the door, but it stuck. He grunted and swore and shook the door. Jane stood motionless, watching the spectacle with a fighting combination of gripping fear and empty resignation. The pub no longer seemed so lovely, things appeared tarnished and broken under the layer of fresh paint. Suddenly, the lock gave way. Jo wiped the sweat from his forehead and stepped clumsily through the doorway.

As they climbed the stairs, Jane's mind returned to the wedding ceremony they had witnessed that afternoon, and her heart began to beat faster and faster. The storm of thoughts and emotions she had held tightly inside since hearing that one short sentence at the reception was growing ready to burst.

For now, Jo was blissfully ignorant of Jane's turmoil. He'd

been in a drunken stupor for most of the journey back and hadn't noticed Jane's distress. Not that he was particularly observant at the best of times. Now it was going to be the worst of times, but all he knew was he needed a piss, so he hurriedly unlocked the room and made a dash for the bathroom, slamming the door after him.

Jane was still in the corridor. She caught her heel in a bare patch of carpet outside a door marked 'Office – Private' and landed hard against the wall as the strap slipped from her heel. The incident didn't seem to attract any attention from other guests. *Were there any other guests?* That question broke her train of thought and brought her temper back under control. Her breathing eased slightly.

She turned into their bedroom and closed the door. Then she was lost for ideas as to what to do next. Her body did its own thing. She sat down on the bed and her arm reached to turn on the bedside lamp. It didn't work. Of course it didn't. Jane's chin dropped to her chest and she hid her face in her hands. Everything was falling apart.

Jo flung the bathroom door open and stumbled back into the room, simultaneously removing his shirt and tie.

'Wasn't that great? Being back with the old crowd again? I feel ten years younger. Never thought Gerry would marry a soldier. Decent bloke though and his mates were a laugh. I was chatting to…'

The sound of Jo's drunken chatting receded into the

distance for Jane as her mind began gaining speed and she reflected on the day's events.

The wedding had been perfect. Gerry looked stunning and Sam so handsome in his uniform. Everyone was so happy for them, and over the moon at the surprise of seeing Sarah again after all the time that had passed. They were even more excited to be introduced to her son. There was something different about Sarah though. She'd been smiling a lot and there were hugs and kisses all round but she didn't have the sparkle in her eye that she used to.

As a group they had never judged each other, and nobody did now. They might have been wondering about who the father was but there were no probing questions being asked about the boy, just a sharing of the sentiment that they felt bad that she'd gone through this life milestone without any of them to lean on. Sarah hadn't wanted to dwell on it, and had turned the attention back to Gerry.

At that point Jo had backed off from the crowd. Jane thought maybe he was afraid she would start feeling broody, when he wasn't ready for kids. People close to Jane had always said that her overthinking would get the better of her, that it would trap her in a corner of her own mind. She said she liked to think things through and be prepared – but her overthinking hadn't helped her prepare for what happened next, and now she was right there in that dirty corner with no way out.

It was one comment. The agony of those few words was excruciating. It was one line from Sarah's sister. Her strained smile had given way to an angry whisper in Jane's ear, 'Don't you think he's got Jo's eyes?'

Jane's mind, heart and soul hit the floor. Her world collapsed in an instant. She had frozen to the spot, while Sarah's sister pushed past her, gripping the boy's hand.

'No, it can't be,' she thought. Surely she would have known, seen the signs at the time. How could they have done this?

After not breathing for what felt like forever she had gasped, instantly sobered. For Gerry's sake she had to keep the internal tsunami still. She spent the next hour at the quiet end of the bar, leaning on the wall for support, and going over and over scenario after scenario, imagining what could have gone on between Jo and Sarah. Ultimately, she was sure it wasn't true, but still her mind whirled.

In their bedroom, Jo was still going on about conversations he'd had and jokes he'd been told.

Jane stood up. She was shaking with rage and hurt. She took a deep breath and interrupted his flow.

'Is there something I should know about you and Sarah?'

Jo was silenced, as if halted in his train of thought by an oncoming juggernaut of shock and fear. Jane could see it on his face: he had thought he was safe.

He swallowed hard and stared ahead of him, not moving.

He didn't look at her. Had he pushed this secret so far to the back of his mind that he thought it was buried forever? Did he think he would be able to keep it quiet indefinitely? Did he think loving Jane was enough to erase the past?

His silence told Jane everything she needed to know and her tears flowed and flowed. She grabbed the car keys and fled the room. Outside, on the other side of the car park, she slumped down on a rickety bench under a flickering orange light and tried to catch her breath. Everything else was in darkness. She could only see clearly the few feet around her, and she felt so alone.

As she calmed, she noticed more of her surroundings. Under her fingers she felt the rough wood of the bench and started picking at the splinters. Her nostrils filled with an acrid combination of metal and decaying vegetation. The stinging nettles were lapping at her ankles in the gentle breeze. She wished she wasn't still in her stupid dress.

'God this place is a dump. I'm in some shitty town in the middle of nowhere, and my husband has a son with a woman who was one of my best friends.' She said it out loud in the hope that doing so would somehow provide an anchor, a starting point in the journey forward. She had no one else to talk to. Her phone was upstairs. What could she do? How could she even start to deal with this?

The sound of footsteps broke the silence. Jane peered into the darkness.

'Jane?' It was Jo's voice, but plaintive like she'd never heard before. 'Jane, I'm so sorry.'

It pulled at Jane's heart. She loved him, and so the pain cut to the bone.

'I can't hear it now. I'm going to sleep in the car,' she said. 'Just leave me alone. Please.'

'No, Jane, I'll sleep in the car. Go back to the room. Try to sleep. We'll get home tomorrow and deal with it together, I promise.' Jo stepped towards Jane to take the keys and as Jane stood he pulled her into his arms. Jane tried to resist and then gave in to the familiar comfort of his embrace. She cried and cried, and tears ran down Jo's face too.

Jane lay in bed and looked for patterns in the cracks of the ceiling. It took all the strength she had left just to lie there. So much had changed in one night. She thought back to the wedding card and 'passionate friends'. Maybe at some level she had always known.

2013

An Equal Failing

by Alice Little

So, I was behind the bar, probably wiping it down or something, like they do in films. That's how I remember it, at least. And this girl walks in. Woman, I should say. She was about my age, maybe a bit older. Twenty-seven? Let's go with that. Though I'd say twenty-five if she asked me to guess. Anyway, she walks in and looks at me, looks up and down the bar as if she'd rather have gone to someone else, sees there's no one else serving, and she orders a white wine.

'House white?' I ask. It's easier to say that than to list all the options. There are seven kinds of white wine here, and most people don't know the difference.

'Sauvignon blanc?' She pronounces it properly – *so*-vignon, not *sav*-ignon, like most people say.

I decide to tease her a little, see if she knows the answer to the next question. 'French or New Zealand?' (As if French is a country, or New Zealand is a nationality. I can't bring myself to say Kiwi.)

'Marlborough?' she asks back, quick as you like. Now I'm the one who's stumped.

'Naturally,' I say, hoping it is.

She nods. 'Medium.'

I take the bottle from the fridge, thanking my stars when I see the correct region printed clearly on the label.

She's not smiling. I don't think she realises I was teasing her. Either that or she's simply not having any of it. She probably thinks I'm chatting her up, but that's not what I meant by it. It's just nice to have people to joke with at the moment. But maybe I should stick to people I know.

Especially so soon after Isabelle's death.

This girl, this woman, is the complete opposite of Isabelle. Izzy wouldn't have known her *so*-vignon from her pinot, let alone her Marlborough from her... whatever. Izzy drank the house white, like everyone else. But there's something about this woman that reminds me of her. Perhaps it's the way she has pulled her hair over her left shoulder (though it's brown, not blonde), or the way she's staring at me now. She takes a sip of wine, as if she's waiting for something.

'Thanks,' I say, hoping it will end the transaction and she'll go and find a seat. *Please don't pull up a bar stool.*

'Aren't you going to charge me?'

'Oh, right.' I tap the till. 'Six-ninety.' *Six-ninety? For one medium glass?* I double check I've not charged for the bottle. But she's taken out a card.

'Contactless?'

I key the price into the machine and hold it out for her.

'Thanks,' she says, and picks up her glass. She steps back,

then pauses. I wait, imagining she's about to give her condolences, though how would she know to do so? *Maybe she knew Izzy?* No, how would someone like her know Izzy?

'Thanks,' she says again, and crosses the room to sit against the wall under the telly.

She takes out her phone, but I can tell she's not really engaging with it. I carry on wiping the bar, collecting empties, filling the dishwasher. She drinks quickly, occasionally checking her watch. Is she waiting for a date? She can't be, she hasn't looked round at the door once, though several people have come in since she sat down. I see her check out the screen above the bar, the one that shows the train times. Maybe she's popped in for a drink while changing trains? But she only looks at it once, as if by accident, then looks away.

I glance at the clock. At eight that bloody woman's going to come and play the piano, like she does every Wednesday. At five-to, the woman with the white wine gets up, returns her empty glass to the bar, says 'Thanks' again, and leaves.

*

A few days later, she's back. She looks tired. Haggard, you might say. Maybe she's just started a new job, moved in nearby, and is trying to make this her local. If she is, she's not trying very hard, sitting by herself like that. Maybe she's waiting for someone to strike up a conversation?

I'm behind the bar again, though David said he didn't

need me tonight. But at the moment I want to keep busy, Mum agreed it would be good for me. I worked here when David and Judith first took over, before I joined the navy, and it's where all my mates come after work, so I'd rather be here than at home by myself. David said I could go if things got a bit much, or I wanted some time to myself. I've got two weeks of leave left after this weekend, and the truth is I'm scared of being on my own. I think too much, and I've done enough crying to last me a lifetime. So now I'm just trying to keep busy. Maybe I should have gone back to base sooner, but I wanted to be here, where she was, where we were.

I decide to be nice to her – to this woman who orders the posh white wine though she knows what it costs, and pays nearly seven pounds a glass without blinking. It's the same bottle I opened for her a couple of nights ago, no one else has had any since. For all David and Judith's craft ales and varieties of wine, most people stick to what they know.

'Have you just moved in round here?' Of course she hasn't. She wouldn't live so close to the station.

'No. I live… nearby.'

I want to ask where, but that would be creepy, so I just say, 'Oh.'

'You're local?' she asks me.

'Yes, but I'm not usually here. I'm in the navy.'

'Wouldn't have thought you needed a second job on that

kind of salary,' she smiles, then looks embarrassed, probably thinking it's rude to talk about money.

'I'm just helping out,' I say. 'David's a mate.' I point vaguely in his direction so she realises I mean the landlord.

She's distracted, looking over at the corner. Is she meeting someone this time? 'Look,' she says, 'could you keep an eye on my drink while I run to the loo? Sorry, I should have gone before I ordered, but I didn't want you to think I wasn't a customer. You know.' It's the most I've yet heard her say.

'Trusting of you,' I say, winking. I cringe: I shouldn't have winked. She doesn't notice though, she's already halfway to the bathroom.

When she comes back, it's as if me looking after her drink has broken the ice, made us friends. She pulls up a bar stool and puts her coat over the back.

'I don't really live near here at all. I came on the train from Radley. I know it's quite far to come for a drink, but I like this pub. It feels welcoming.'

'Have you been here before, then? Before the other night, I mean.'

She looks down at her glass, avoiding meeting my eye. 'No, but I heard about this place, and it sounded like the people might be... understanding.'

'Understanding...?' I start to ask, then stop myself. I think I know what she means. How else would she have heard about the Railway Inn? It has been on TV for a fortnight, since Isabelle's death: the backdrop to interviews with her neighbours and friends, her uncle and, of course, her fiancé.

She must have known Izzy. Somehow. Or maybe she lost someone herself, somewhere else – in the place her accent is from, where wine costing six-ninety a glass is normal.

If she's seen the pub on TV, then she knows who I am, too.

'I'm Tom,' I say, to save her having to pretend she doesn't already know my name.

'Amelia,' she says, and holds out her hand over the bar.

*

She's back again the very next day, a Saturday. I'm glad, because David'll get annoyed if we have to bin half a bottle of expensive wine, or sell it as house white. She's brought a friend this time. A redhead who orders a rum and coke. They sit together at the table under the telly. It's where Isabelle used to sit when she wanted to be noticed, before we got together – when I was just another barman, playing pool with my mates on my breaks and stealing glances at the pretty girls while pretending to read the news subtitles.

But these girls – sorry, women – aren't gossiping like Izzy and her mates used to, leaning close across the table and then screaming with laughter. The redhead is loud, she's drinking quickly, and comes to the bar for a top-up solo round before Amelia has finished her wine. Amelia is sitting up very straight, almost sternly, as if she's trying not to be associated with her friend. If you asked me, I'd have said they weren't really friends at all, that Amelia brought the redhead along to see if she would fit in here, in this welcoming and understanding pub, and had concluded that she wouldn't – and was regretting bringing her.

But who am I to judge who people should be friends with? I don't know either of them. But, well, I just get this vibe from Amelia. Like she's someone I want to hang out with more, someone who would listen and understand. Maybe it's the same feeling she gets in this pub.

God, pretty weird to be thinking like this about another woman when my fiancée died only two weeks ago. Not just died – when my fiancée was *killed* two weeks ago. By person or persons as yet unknown, that's what the police said. *As yet.* They found her drowned in the lake, where people walk their dogs at weekends. Lying face down in the shallows, not like she fell off a dinghy or something, more like someone knocked her out and left her there, or held her head under.

I feel sick. I shouldn't let these thoughts come. *Even though they're all true.* I nip out the back for a cigarette. Only I don't smoke anymore, not since I've been in the navy – you can't smoke on a submarine – so I just sit on the wall at the edge of the car park, my feet kicking against the bricks, facing the road, and wait for the feeling to pass.

A gentle hand pulls my shoulder backwards, and my arms flail as I attempt to stop myself falling. 'What the–'

'Sorry.' She's embarrassed. Amelia. 'It was a joke. Like those team-building exercises where you have to fall into someone's arms. Sorry, I shouldn't have. I misjudged.'

'Oh. No worries.' But my heart is pounding.

'Anyway, you shouldn't trust anybody till you know them.' She laughs. 'Especially people you go on team-building exercises with.' She leans on the wall next to me.

'Is that who you're with tonight, a colleague?'

'Sort of. I'm freelance, so's she. We're in the same line of work.'

I don't want to ask what she does, so I say, 'Did she go home?'

'Yes. I said I had to get the train at half past. She lives nearby, so she's walking.'

'I take it you *don't* have to get the train at half past?' There was something in the way she'd said it.

She smiles at me. Then, taking the hint, jumps up onto the wall. She rubs the grit off her palm.

'So, you don't trust anyone, then?' I ask. We're back to teasing.

'Well, the way I see it, it's a sliding scale. You have to work out where to draw the line: you can't just trust everyone, just like you can't go through life trusting no one. An equal failing, my mum says: it's as equal a failing to trust nobody as to trust everybody. You have to get to know people a bit before you can decide.'

'Right.' This is all getting a bit deep for me.

'But, well…'

Ah, here we go, the thing she actually wants to say. *Is it about Izzy?* I take a deep breath and steel myself.

'I've been wondering recently, how well you have to know someone before you can really trust them.'

'Yeah?' *Had I really known Izzy?* I didn't like to think about it. There was no way to be sure now. *Did I trust Izzy?* I had worked really hard on that, after her one-night stand with that guy from work. *Rick.* I met him once at a Christmas party, before it happened. We had been through six months of heart breaking and mending, but we were getting there. I wouldn't have proposed if I hadn't trusted her again afterwards. 'So what made you think about all this?'

'Sorry, it's a bit heavy. I guess I've just been having trouble trusting… people recently.' She looks sideways at me, and for a minute I think she's going to try and kiss me. I feel like I'm fifteen again, sitting with Sarah Bell on the school bus, only without the other kids egging us on.

She shivers.

'Do you want to go in?'

'In a minute.'

She is leaning on her hands, sitting on the wall, her

shoulders hunched up around her ears for warmth. I don't know why I do it, but I let my knuckles rest on the back of her hand between us on the wall. It's not like I'm holding her hand, and I didn't mean it like that anyway. I could tell she was struggling with something – and I felt exactly the same, only about Isabelle. But, it was weird: I wasn't sure if what I was doing was wrong.

Is it still cheating when your partner is no longer alive?

Amelia doesn't move. I take my hand back. We remain for a few minutes more, as if we're both making clear that it's not my action that's made us go back inside.

'Do you want another drink?' I ask.

'Sure, why not?' She jumps down from the wall.

I pour out the last of the bottle for her. It's more than a medium glass, but I don't charge her for it. David would have written it off anyway, on the fourth day.

*

The following week is Isabelle's funeral, and I'm relieved that I don't see Amelia at the pub. The wake is at Izzy's mum's place, down the road, and people go off to the Railway Inn when they feel they should leave Tracy to herself. I stay behind to help clear up, and we watch a film together and both cry a bit.

I'm next working behind the bar (volunteering, I suppose) the Tuesday after. Now that the funeral has happened, it's business as usual here. The local tragedy is over. Back to normal. But for me it will never be the same again. I've got till the end of the week on leave, then I'm back to base at the weekend. I'm not sure I'm ready, but I won't know unless I try.

The TV is back on the news when I arrive – it's been on the sports channel for the last couple of weeks, even though there's been bugger all going on, so that I didn't have to keep seeing the rolling coverage of the police investigation on the local programme. They never found anything new, anyway, so there wasn't much point in following the news. The officers said they'd call if there were any developments.

Amelia comes in just after six. It's dark already. She's got pink cheeks, and I wonder if she's come from somewhere else rather than straight off the train.

'Sav-blanc?' I ask, reaching for the fridge door.

'Actually, I can't stay long. I just thought I'd come in and say hello, since I was nearby.'

'Oh, right.' Why would she be nearby if she wasn't coming here? Does she just want to chat? David comes past at that moment and notices me being a bit awkward.

'It's quiet, Tom, you can go for a walk and come back in a bit, lad.'

I smile my thanks. I hope he doesn't think we're dating. I wouldn't replace Izzy so quickly. I haven't even decided if I should ever replace her: if we'd been married as we planned, I'd never have gone out with another woman again.

'Left or right?' I ask when we get to the pavement. The hanging baskets, devoid of life, are swinging in the chill breeze. Judith said we should have brought them in for the winter, but somehow they're still here in February.

'Let's just sit. I can get the train in twenty minutes.'

We sit on the wall again. She keeps looking across the road at the station, though she knows the timetable. Perhaps she's expecting to see someone. It's almost as if she's afraid of someone seeing her. She shudders.

'Why don't we...' I begin. 'Look, don't think me too forward or anything, but that's my house over there. If you're cold we can just wait inside.'

She looks up the road at the house. I wish I'd brought the bins in this morning.

'I thought you were in the navy, don't you live on base?'

'It's my mum's house. But she's at work till nine.'

Amelia nods. Once inside, she seems to collapse in on herself. 'Cup of tea?' I try, hovering in the doorway, but it's clearly not the time for that. Something must have happened.

'There's something I wanted to talk to you about.'

Oh God, she's going to tell me she likes me. Now is not the time. I wonder how I can head her off without seeming rude. Maybe in a few months, or a year, I would be glad to think about someone else, but not yet. I can't deal with it now, less than a week after Isabelle's funeral.

'It's about Isabelle Jenkins,' she says. It knocks the wind right out of me. I sit down on the armchair.

'What– what about her?' I manage. *Please don't tell me Amelia's a stalker, that she was only interested in talking to me because I was on the telly.*

Or – shit – could it have been her? Could Amelia have killed Isabelle? And I've let her get close to me, and brought her into my house. Shit. No, that doesn't make sense. She can't be.

'I was there, the day she was found.'

…Or a reporter – going to print that I'm chatting up women in pubs before my fiancée is cold in the ground? No, that doesn't feel right either. But then, she did ask me whether I trusted her.

'Say something,' she prompts.

'I'm… I don't understand what you mean,' I say. 'In what capacity…' *Fuck, who am I? 'In what capacity'?* 'Why were you there when she was found?'

'Oh. Sorry. I see.' Our eyes meet for the first time. 'I'm the one who found her.'

Shit. She'd been there. She had seen Isabelle in the water. She was there!

'I thought it was someone walking their dog,' I say. *Of all the stupid things to say.*

'Yes. I was walking my dog.'

I laugh then. I can't help it. I start with a snicker, and then a belly laugh erupts from me. I think I must have been holding my breath.

She smiles a little, but she's obviously not sure what's going on, whether she's allowed in on the joke, or whether it's really funny at all. I had been imagining a fat old biddy with a little terrier, that was all. I'd never thought to ask the police what sort of person it was or what sort of dog. For some reason it now seems like something I'd like to know, to get the picture right in my mind.

'He's a cocker spaniel,' she says when I ask, clearly bemused by the question.

I take a few deep breaths and calm myself down. 'Sorry.'

'That's OK.' She looks like she's about to cry. I hadn't meant to upset her.

'I'd imagined it differently,' I try to explain. Suddenly serious, I ask, 'Is that why you came to the pub that first time? Like, because Isabelle was here.'

'Yes,' she says. 'But I don't want you to think I'm some kind of... *tourist*. I just... felt involved. I didn't mean for us to get chatting. It's not like I'm trying to replace her, or become her, or anything like that. I mean, I'm married.'

This is almost as shocking as the revelation that she'd been there that day. Maybe more so. *Why 'more so'? What could be worse than...*

'Why are you telling me all this? Have you had your fun?' I'm angry now. 'Is that why you brought your friend? To show her where all the grieving people were?'

'No,' she looks taken aback. 'I wanted to be there for myself... I just... thought it looked weird coming on my own. I didn't want people to ask questions about why I was there. And I didn't want to tell you all of this, it's just that I need to tell you so I can... tell you something else.'

I wait. I become aware that we're in my mum's house. I don't want her there anymore.

'It's my husband,' she says.

'What is?'

'Him and Isabelle... I think they might have been having an affair. Or... that he might have...'

It's that 'or' that gets me. *What could be worse than infidelity? I know what could be worse.*

'Get out!' I shout. I can't stand, but point towards the door.

She looks shocked at my raised voice, but she obeys, rising shakily. She puts her hand in her bag and pulls out a business card.

'Look, here's my number,' she says, putting the card on the coffee table. 'I'd like to tell you what made me think... when you're ready.' She pulls the front door shut behind her.

I don't watch her go, but a few minutes later I see the train pull in at the station, and feel relief that it will carry her away from me.

*

The thing is, she did have a one-night stand before.

I can't get this thought out of my mind. It goes round and round all night.

Mum comes back from work, but I'm already in bed. She looks in on me around midnight but I don't open my eyes. She goes back downstairs, and I hear the laughter track from the telly.

Isabelle promised it was the only time. The guy, Rick, texted her later, after she had told me all about it – and I wondered if it had gone on longer than she'd been prepared to admit. We were doing so well, rebuilding trust, working through our issues, talking and talking. I proposed to her, and she said yes, and it felt like our future was set. We were sorted. Nothing could ever come between us now.

Had she done it again?

Had it resulted in her death?

I wouldn't blame her for wanting more, not entirely: I'm away for so long at a time on the boat. I promised to leave the navy when we had our first child – she said she wanted that to be soon. I have to give a year's notice, so I promised to do it straight after the wedding. I smile to myself as I realise I might have ended up working in the pub, just like I am now, but the smile fades when I remember that in that image it's because we're together, not because she's died. Now there's no point giving notice. There won't be a baby, there won't be a wedding. There's no Isabelle.

But we'd only just got engaged. She seemed so happy. Why would she have an affair *now*?

But was it now? I need to know. It's almost three in the morning. I get out of bed and go downstairs to find Amelia's card. Mum hasn't moved it.

I compose the text four times before I hit send. 'It's Tom. I just want to know, when do you think it was?' I can't write the word 'affair'. I can't write Isabelle's name.

A reply comes straight away. 'You can't sleep either, huh?' Then a more serious reply: 'I don't know. Recently. Within the last six months.'

'What made you think it?'

'His behaviour changed. What's her number? I can check his phone while he's asleep.'

It felt like a betrayal to type that familiar string of digits.

'Nothing there. But he might have a second phone.' Then: 'Can I come over tomorrow? It's hard to text it, but there are things about him… I'd rather tell you in person.'

I say she can come at six.

She arrives the next evening looking sheepish. She says she doesn't want a cup of tea. She sits in the same seat as yesterday.

Her explanation has barely begun ('It's hard to describe, it's a feeling more than anything, but a couple of times…') when my phone rings. I'm almost relieved: I don't think I want to hear what she has to say.

'I'm sorry, David needs me at the pub.'

'I thought you didn't actually work there.'

'I don't get paid, but he's short-staffed tonight, and he's a mate, so. You can come with me if you like.'

'We can't really talk there, though.'

'You can come back tomorrow?'

'I'm not sure I want to be at home tonight, with…'

'Oh, OK. Well.' I shrug. I feel less protective of her now than I did before the funeral. I'm more wary of the power she has to hurt me – by tainting my memory of Izzy.

At the Inn, she sits on a stool, cradling a glass of wine. (I gave her the house white this time, I didn't want to charge her, and I can't give her the good stuff for free. She doesn't seem to notice.)

It's funny, even though I know she's married, and I realise she's not interested in me *that way* – this is all about Isabelle, not me – I still have the feeling she's *looking* at me: smiling when I drop things, watching me as I walk away, averting her gaze when I'm facing her.

I try not to meet her eye too often, though she is very pretty. So I look at the telly instead. The news is on, and for a second I think they're back by the lake again. They *are* back by the lake. It's old footage from the day. *That day.* And then it cuts to a reporter, and the banner along the bottom of the screen says 'New developments in drowning case, arrest made'.

'Turn it up!' I shout at David, and Amelia looks up in surprise. In his haste, David drops the remote under the bar, then lunges across the room to turn the volume up on the set. Everyone is looking at the screen. I can't tear my eyes away. *Who is it?*

The screen shows officers outside a house. A man is being taken away in handcuffs. It's Rick.

I look at Amelia. She looks confused. 'It's not him,' she says. Then more confidently, 'It's not him.' She almost smiles.

But it is him. It's Isabelle's murderer.

My phone is ringing. It's the number of the detectives' office. Amelia has put her coat on, and is reaching for my arm. She guides me to the door, and I take the call.

2015

Karaoke Surprise

by Jane Andrews

Although I know of the Railway Inn, I've only ever been in once before this evening, so I feel a little apprehensive as I push open the door and make my way inside. I suppose you could say that I'm on a blind date, although it's more of a second date with someone I just happened to bump into by chance a few days ago, when I spontaneously decided to treat myself to breakfast in here after I did my weekly shop. Other people had been telling me for ages that I should try this place out – it's been under new management since the new year, and the menu is full of locally-sourced organic meat – but since my last, disastrous, relationship was with a vegan, there wasn't much opportunity to sit down with a plate of sausage, bacon and eggs, so I was making up for lost time.

The pub wasn't too busy, and only half the tables were occupied, even though it was a Saturday morning, when you might have expected to see lots of families. Since it was my first time, I wasn't quite sure of the system – did I find a table first, I wondered, or would I be given a wooden spoon with a number on it? – I wandered up to the bar and waited to be served, giving me plenty of time to study the blackboard with the 'Railway Breakfast' menu. I couldn't help glancing around as I did so and feeling slightly uncomfortable when I realised that I seemed to be the only single female in the establishment. However, that didn't stop me ordering a mug of tea and a standard cooked breakfast. I don't normally pig out in the morning, but having come in spontaneously, I decided this should be a celebration of my recent pay rise at work – even if it was only an extra thirty or so pounds a month.

The barmaid who served me was warm and friendly, about my age, with a blonde ponytail and gypsy earrings. When it was my turn to be served, I flashed her a dazzling smile and asked for extra crispy bacon and well-done sausages. 'They're not chipolatas, are they?' I enquired. 'Only I like really big sausages.'

A stranger standing beside me snorted and I blushed as I realised that what I'd said could be open to misinterpretation. Then I took a quick look at him: medium height, brown hair, no wedding ring. He gave me a disarming grin. 'I was about to ask for one myself,' he quipped, 'but I'm afraid you might read something into it now!'

I assured him this wasn't the case and picked up my drink, searching for an empty table. My companion did the same. Somehow, in the time I'd been standing at the bar, the pub had filled up and there was now only one unoccupied table in the whole room. I hesitated, not wanting to seem rude by taking the last available spot, but the friendly guy spoke up.

'Shall we sit there?' he asked. 'Unless you'd rather be on your own?'

As we sat and chatted, over endless refillable cups of tea once the breakfasts were demolished, I learnt that his name was Adam, he worked in IT and that he'd just come out of a long-term relationship.

'What happened?' I asked sympathetically.

Adam shrugged. 'We both wanted different things: I wanted to settle down and she just wanted a good time.'

I regarded him critically. While not as breathtakingly gorgeous as Brad Pitt or David Beckham, Adam was nevertheless still a good-looking guy. The faded jeans he was wearing moulded themselves to his legs and bum – yes, I had a good look when we were standing at the bar – and his dark brown hair and khaki-coloured eyes were a pretty potent combination. I decided that I certainly wouldn't be saying no if he asked me out on a date.

In case you think I'm shallow, mentioning Adam's physical attributes rather than his intellect or personality, don't worry – we talked for hours. (One hour and thirty-seven minutes, to be precise.) I learnt that he's into Biffy Clyro, Everything Everything and Porcupine Tree (I'd heard of the first two bands but couldn't name any of their songs); and I told him about my penchant for Lana del Ray and Kate Bush, even admitting to channelling Kate for the odd karaoke performance.

His eyes lit up when I mentioned karaoke. 'There's a karaoke night here this Tuesday,' he said eagerly. 'It's usually a general open mic night, but once a month they do karaoke instead. We should go.'

I couldn't believe it was all happening so fast: I'm not usually that lucky with men. And, OK, I'll admit it, I was quite excited by the prospect of karaoke too.

We chatted a while longer, fine tuning details, making sure we both liked each other as much as we thought we did. We swapped mobile numbers and I was surprised when he pulled a bog-standard Nokia out of his pocket to add my details into his address book.

'I lost my iPhone last week,' he told me. 'It's covered by insurance, but until I get a replacement, I'm stuck with this old one.'

I really didn't mind: after some of the guys I've dated, who were obsessed with having the latest this or the newest that, finding someone who wasn't a techno-nerd seemed like a breath of fresh air.

Finally, after several more drinks – by this time noon had struck and we'd moved on from the breakfast mugs of tea and started on the wine – and a detailed breakdown of where we went to school, what we did for A Levels, and where our ideal holiday destination would be, we reluctantly said goodbye until Tuesday. If you must know, I was quite relieved to have a few days to myself before the big night: it would take me until then to get myself properly date-ready, anyway, seeing as my legs hadn't seen a razor since the previous September and my bikini line currently resembled Epping Forest. (Not that I was intending to sleep with him on Tuesday, but a girl likes to know she's prepared.)

*

So now it's Tuesday and I'm entering the Railway Inn for the second time – I suppose it's a fitting venue, considering this is where we met. I've taken care with my appearance, mindful that, when we ate breakfast together, Adam saw me with my hair scraped back in a ponytail, wearing old jeans and a faded top. I've pulled out all the stops now, having chosen a denim miniskirt that draws attention to my legs, and letting my newly washed hair cascade over my shoulders. I've even applied smoky grey eyeshadow that accentuates my eyes, making them a more intense shade of brown. And, although he's not going to see it tonight, I'm wearing sexy underwear: a matching black lace combination of bra and G-string, which is totally unlike my everyday choice of support bra and granny knickers.

Adam looks to have made an effort too: he's in a white shirt and black jeans, with Terminator harness boots, and he's left enough buttons undone on his shirt to lend him a

Byronic quality. My pulse quickens as I look at him, and I begin to wonder if he might actually get to see my new underwear after all.

For the first few minutes, we are polite and stilted, two strangers unsure of what to say to each other. It is as if the mammoth heart-to-heart over breakfast and the couple of flirty texts we've exchanged with each other since belonged to someone else. Then, gradually, we begin to unwind, alcohol loosening our tongues and relaxing our body language. We order food – a chicken burger for me and a curry for him, with a bowl of chips to share – and, when our fingers collide, reaching for the mayonnaise, we allow the moment to last, savouring the thrill of touching each other, retaining eye contact for longer than is strictly necessary.

The karaoke begins and it is truly and tackily terrible. The first victim is a young lad of about twenty who can't sing at all – I suspect his mates have dared him to do it, and Adam agrees. After he has murdered 'Don't Stop Believing', a rather overweight woman in her fifties takes the stage. Her statuesque proportions suggest that she might have an amazing set of lungs, like a good old-fashioned opera singer, but instead her voice is thin and reedy, and the lyrics to 'I Will Always Love You' are lost without a trace.

Adam looks at me and shakes his head. 'Unbelievable!' he mutters. 'Why do people like that insist on big power ballads when they can't even hold a tune?'

I'm with him on that one: this is beginning to feel like one of the outtakes episodes of *The X Factor*, where they only show you the people who are awful.

'You should get up and show them how it's done,' I say. This isn't as random as it sounds, he's already told me he used to be in a band and that he and his ex performed lots of karaoke together.

'OK,' he says, accepting my challenge, 'you're on – but I expect to see you up there doing your Kate Bush next!'

He disappears from the table, making his way towards the stage. I have to sit through a mother and daughter duet of 'I Know Him So Well' (creepy, or what?) and another nervous young man singing 'Blue Suede Shoes' before Adam finally gets his turn, but when I hear him, I know it was worth waiting for.

Adam has chosen an obscure Bob Dylan number, 'Is Your Love In Vain?', but, unlike Dylan, he can actually sing. His voice is soulfully husky yet powerful; the room goes quiet once he gets into his stride. The lyrics are mesmerising too: a heartfelt plea to the woman he loves, asking her whether or not she's just using him. I listen, spellbound. There's so much hurt and raw emotion in his tone: he must be thinking about his ex and the way she hurt him.

Adam finishes the song to rapturous applause and makes his way back to our table. 'That was incredible,' I say earnestly, wondering how my pathetic attempt to cover Kate

Bush can ever compare to that.

He gives a modest, self-deprecating smile. 'It's not the first time I've sung that song.'

If I had any doubts about the two of us before, they've totally vanished now. I suddenly understand how groupies feel, because after hearing Adam sing like that I'd follow him anywhere, do anything.

His eyes meet mine and he reaches across the table to take my hand in his. 'You don't have to do your Kate Bush tonight,' he says. 'We could just go back to your place instead.'

It's tempting – more than tempting. In fact, I'm on the verge of taking out my phone and calling us a cab when a hand falls on the back of my shoulder and a voice I don't recognise shrieks, 'Kate! I thought you said you and Adam couldn't make it tonight.'

I spin round, thinking how weird it is that I'm being called Kate when I haven't even got up to sing yet, and the stranger's face registers surprise. 'Sorry! You're not Kate. But I thought….' Then her eyes take in Adam and she stares at me accusingly. 'What are you doing with my best friend's boyfriend?'

Boyfriend? I gaze at Adam in shock, willing him to tell me that this other girl has got it wrong. Instead, he looks guilty, shifty. He's been caught out and he knows it.

'You said you'd split up with your girlfriend….' I can't

believe that someone would do this to me. How dare he lie like that? I'd been on the verge of sleeping with him too.

'It's complicated….' Adam looks nervous, but this friend of Kate's isn't letting him off the hook.

'You told her you were working late,' she declares, watching his face to see if he'll try to deny it. 'I messaged her earlier to see if the two of you were coming out tonight and she said you were working and you'd asked her to stay in and carry on with the decorating for you.'

'It's not like that,' Adam protests. 'I *was* working late, but then things changed and I just popped in here for a quick drink and got chatting to Lucy at the bar. I've never seen her before tonight.'

He looks at me, appealing, begging me to back up his story, but I've had enough. 'I don't go out with people who're already taken,' I tell him bluntly. 'You had several hours to tell me about Kate last Saturday, when we had breakfast together, but you chose not to.'

'I forgot.' Even Adam must know that this excuse is pathetically flimsy.

'Well, you'd better forget my number too,' I order him brusquely, rising to my feet in front of a startled – what *is* this stranger's name? 'I don't want to hear from you again, Adam – not that you'll have the chance to misbehave when your girlfriend's friend–'

'Julie,' the friend adds obligingly.

'–when Julie tells her what you've been up to.'

By now I'm so angry that I feel like grabbing his pint and pouring it over his head, but I don't. Adam will have to face the wrath of Kate when he gets home: I'll let her tear him to shreds instead.

I seize my jacket and my phone and begin to stalk out of the pub. At least I've found out now, rather than later. No wonder he only had a crappy Nokia – it must be his secret phone for making dates with women behind his girlfriend's back. And based on his pathetic excuse to me and Julie, I have a feeling that Adam would have been only too ready to 'forget' to tell Kate that he was seeing someone else while she was slaving away with the decorating.

This evening's not turned out the way I planned, but I suppose I've given the locals something to talk about.

That's when the full consequences hit me – the Railway Inn's a lovely pub, but after tonight I don't think I'll ever be able to show my face in there again.

2016

Another Railway Town

by Mike Evis

I'm always drawn to railway towns. There's something about them. Easy to get to – and easy to get away from. If I had a car, then it'd be motorway towns. But there's a problem with that: a car comes with a registration number; it can be traced. On the railway you're anonymous, untraceable.

See, I don't like being tied down. Relationships, friendships – people get to know too much about you. Once that happens you're not free anymore. I pick up the warning signs and I start to get restless. I feel an itch, an irresistible urge to be elsewhere. It might be something as simple as seeing a street once too often, or the sight of the wallpaper in my flat. Or just a sense of boredom, knowing there is another world out there to discover. It's hard to explain. Other people don't feel like this, but I do. It's like Mary Poppins when she says, 'I'll stay till the wind changes.' That's how it is. I'm a drifter, always have been. Nothing could ever make me change my ways, could it?

That's what I was thinking about that night as I sat, frustrated, in the Railway Inn. Don't get me wrong, I'm sure it's a fine pub, it's just that I was on my second pint, and by then I should have been halfway to Bristol. I shouldn't have been there at all. I felt in my back pocket once more, making sure the ticket to Plymouth was still there.

*

It had all gone wrong when I got to the station. The whole place was deserted: no one on the platform, no one in the waiting room, and no one in the ticket hall. Granted, it's never that busy that sort of time, and it was a cold April night, the wind making the station signs swing, but you'd have thought there'd be someone catching a train. Instead, you might as well have had tumbleweed blowing along the platform. Well, that was all right, it meant no one would spot me. I'd planned it so I wouldn't be hanging about too long, arriving with only ten minutes to spare. They'd all be down at the Half Moon Inn for the quiz night; by the time any of them realised, I'd be miles away. That was the plan.

I hadn't answered my phone for three days. I always spend the last few days disengaging completely: I don't see anyone, I avoid all the usual places, I don't answer the door, and then my head is in the right space when I leave town.

Sitting on the desolate platform, I took my phone out of my pocket. All those missed calls from Holly, the last one only ten minutes ago. A text too. 'Nick, I'm worried about you. Where are you? Please, please call me. H x'. It couldn't be helped. I levered the case apart, prised the SIM card out, then walked up to a bin and tossed the phone in. It made a much louder crash than I expected when it hit the bottom.

Then I tossed the card onto the gravel between the tracks, hoping it would slip between the gaps. Annoyingly, it lay right on the top. How likely was that? Quickly I jumped down onto the track, landing awkwardly, and pushed it beneath the stones. Now I was untraceable.

My old life was coming to an end. Freedom beckoned.

'Hey!' shouted a gruff voice, as I heaved myself back up. 'Get off the line! Don't you know how dangerous that is?'

'Sorry,' I muttered sheepishly as a railwayman in a yellow hi-vis jacket plodded up. 'I dropped something.'

'You should get us to pick it up, sir. You could get killed. That's the live rail there. Where are you travelling to?'

I thought quickly. There's little risk, but it's best not to leave a trace. Just in case.

'Exeter,' I said. It was the same train, but if anyone did nose around afterwards it'd be enough to throw them off the scent. Not that anyone would ever check. I hadn't killed anyone, I hadn't committed a crime. No one would care. And the police aren't interested in missing persons provided they're an adult.

He shook his head. 'There's been an incident. All lines out of London shut at the moment.'

'What? How long for?'

'Can't say.' He looked thoughtful. 'Your best bet's to wait and listen for announcements.'

'But I've got to get away tonight. Bloody hell.'

I felt the walls closing in. I struggled to breathe. I'd never had anything like this before, my escape abruptly halted at the last minute.

He shrugged.

'Why don't you go over to the Railway Inn across the way? You can have a drink while you're waiting. It'll be more comfortable than sitting around here. You won't miss your train. They've got their own screen showing the train times.'

I would get out. I had to. I just had to hope I wasn't held up too long.

*

So, I slouched across the road to the Railway Inn. He was right, if I had to wait, this was a much better place than that windswept railway platform. I was just irritated that I couldn't be on the move straight away.

'Another one,' said an old man sitting at the bar as I pushed the door aside. 'Good for trade, eh, when the trains are messed up, eh, Trudy?'

'Can't deny it,' said the barmaid, a woman in her early thirties with a blonde ponytail that betrayed dark roots. Her huge hoop earrings jingled slightly as she pulled a pint.

I stood about six feet inside, taking in my surroundings. A plush, new-looking red carpet under my feet, with bare, polished wooden flooring nearer the bar, and lots of brass work in and around the counter. There were chalked signs everywhere saying things like 'We've got a true passion for our food and drink – we're sure you can tell!!'

In the corner sat a group of six or seven people of widely disparate ages, spread over several tables and writing away in notebooks, a few of them hunched over laptops. One table had a small sign on it: 'Write Club'. None of them were talking. What were they? Some sort of remedial group learning to write? The speed at which they were scribbling away or typing belied that thought; they looked a bit too quick. Were they studying the people in the pub, I wondered? They wouldn't have much to go on with me, that was for sure. That's the trouble with this life I lead. Trust no one, suspect all.

I walked to the bar and peered at the pumps, as the barmaid gave me a smile. 'Grumpy Railwayman and Signal Failure are off tonight – rather appropriate, isn't it? You another one waiting for a train?'

'Yeah.'

'Where you going then?'

'Bristol,' I said.

We both looked over at the screen by the side of the bar. Every single train had the word 'Delayed' next to it.

'Don't look good, does it?' she said.

'No,' I muttered.

I sat down at a small table by the window, with a view of the bar and its display screen. From there I couldn't read it properly, but I'd soon see if anything changed.

I was travelling light. I'd left a few odds and ends at the flat – a couple of old magazines, and half a dozen paperbacks I'd picked up from charity shops, plus an old radio I'd had for a while that had packed in.

Otherwise, all my worldly possessions fitted into a rucksack, which was on the floor by my side. I like travelling light. If you acquire too much stuff, it ties you down. If I really wanted to be pretentious I'd come out with some crap about how I was really into one of those Eastern religions, something like Buddhism, say, and how a lack of material possessions is a good thing for the soul. But it's really so I can move on again every six months.

'What about this referendum,' the old man at the bar called across to the barmaid. 'What do you reckon to that then?'

'What, the EU one?' she said, looking up as she polished a glass. 'I dunno really. Suppose I'll probably vote leave.'

I definitely won't be voting. Even if I wanted to, I'm never around long enough to get on the electoral register.

I sipped my pint. This wasn't a bad pub, even if all those signs talking about 'passion' and 'enthusiasm' got on your wick after a while – and the longer I sat here, the more of them I noticed. 'Got a passion for beer – you'll love ours!!' and 'Enthusiastic about pubs? Why not work in one? Ask us about bar vacancies!' I almost groaned aloud when I saw one reading 'We've a fantastic collection of spirits – plus a

Victorian ghost!' Doesn't every pub this age have one? At least the place was reasonably smart and clean. The upholstery wasn't ripped, the carpet was new, not like the Half Moon where the stains on the tables might as well have been there since Queen Victoria was a baby, and the carpet was so threadbare in places you could see the floorboards underneath. All right, the upright piano over in the corner here looked a bit tattered, but how often do you see a piano in a pub these days? It lent the place a certain charm. Though I did pray no one was going to walk in and start murdering some tune or other. It's the sort of thing some drunk, convinced he's a virtuoso, would do.

I began to relax, slumping back into the cushioned seat. I wasn't going to worry about this setback. I'd have another pint, and then I'd be on my way. I simply had to sit tight.

And then I started mulling over things: the gang, Holly, everything I'd be leaving. Maybe this setback was a sign? Puzzling, because that's something I've never done before, dwelling on things like that – perhaps it was the enforced hold up? Or maybe it was because this time I'd stayed for longer: nine or ten months. Too long; I usually move on after six at the most. As I took another draught of my pint, my thoughts drifted to Holly. Holly, with her elfin hair and blue eyes. Holly and that night in the Market Tavern last week. She had no inkling I was leaving, none at all.

*

The Market Tavern was our pub, where we wouldn't bump into the usual crowd. We could be on our own there, they always went to the Half Moon. We had a meal, and then settled back for a few drinks.

By the window in the other corner, partly illuminated by a street light across the street, a couple in their late twenties sat, elbows supporting their faces as they gazed at each other, lost in a world apart, with no thought of anyone else. I couldn't help staring at them. I was surprised to find I was almost jealous. But I'd already bought my ticket to Plymouth, I would be gone within a week. Of course, I wasn't enough of a bastard to say anything to Holly.

As she snuggled up to me in our corner, we must have looked like love's great dream. If you didn't know the score, that is.

'Nick, do you think we'll last?' she asked quietly.

'Why not?' I said, feeling that knife twist deep inside me. That's why I'm always moving on. People get too close to you, they start to know too much, they can hurt you. So I make a rule – if anyone starts to get too close, really close, it's time to go. And it was getting to the point where, if I stayed longer, Holly would really sink her claws into me. And I couldn't have that.

'I can't believe how quickly it's developed,' she said. 'Our... relationship, I mean.'

'Nor me,' I said, idly running my hand along her arm, and

sighing heavily.

'Why are you sighing?'

'Oh, just… this is so perfect.'

We kissed, I knew what I'd be missing, but that was the way it had to be. I never say goodbye. It's easier like that; you can just imagine the scenes. Once I tried to avoid any entanglement. But I'm not a monk. You can't live that way.

*

The trains still weren't running. I tried to dismiss thoughts of Holly. What was happening to me? I had never felt like this before. I was determined not to change my mind and stay. I couldn't do that, could I?

I felt a chill, colder than the piercing wind outside, go right through me, and I shivered. Soon this will all be over, I thought. Once you're on that train it will be done. I calmed down. Another pint – that was the answer. It wasn't as if the railway station was far away.

I started to get hungry, what with the smell of food, and the barmaid wafting past with hot plates every now and again, but it was well gone nine o'clock now, and the barmaid, in her white blouse and black trousers, came past without food this time, and started to wipe the chalk off the specials board. No matter, it was all expensive gastro pub stuff. The starters were what I'd normally pay for a main course. And as for the main meals – twenty pounds for an 'artisan steak'?

As the barmaid reached up to wipe the last few menu items off the board, her blouse pulled up at the back, providing a glimpse of bare flesh. It was as if she felt my gaze; she turned and smiled. Caught out, I twisted quickly away, a strange half-pang of regret coming over me.

Now she was squeakily chalking up another notice: DARTS MATCH THIS SATURDAY, and MONDAY IS QUIZ NIGHT AT THE RAILWAY; why didn't we ever come here instead? But then the Half Moon was like a second home. That's how I met my gang – Holly, Becki, Tom, and Phil. I would miss them, but you can't get attached. I remembered the open mic night too, and that old bloke who always turned up to play his mouth organ. No one had the heart to turn him away. There was usually a run for the bar when he got behind the microphone. I laughed to think of it.

'Do you think he's playing for money?' I asked Holly one night.

'What, to make him stop?' she giggled, and as I laughed I saw the way she smiled, with her whole face. Even her eyes were grinning at me, and something happened in that moment, though it was a long time before I did anything about it. Or rather, she did. Because I never get attached. Never.

Well, what did any of it matter now? It would be another memory soon, quickly fading once I was out of here. My watch showed 9:45. I sipped my beer.

Then things went from bad to worse.

*

'Nick!' It was Becki, bursting through the door of the Railway Inn. Everyone, even the writing group, looked up. 'Christ, I've looked all over for you. Why weren't you at quiz night? You never miss that. Sat here by yourself when you could be down at the Half Moon?' She shook her head in disbelief.

Her voice rang round the whole pub. 'God, am I glad I found you!' She stopped, her lip quivering, her head bobbing slightly as if there were things she had to say, but couldn't find the words. For an instant she stood motionless in front of the table, towering over me, her hands on her hips.

Bugger, I thought. What bad luck. If that train had been on time, I'd be long gone. Now I sensed the cage doors springing shut against me. I was caught.

She sat down solidly on the chair opposite, but as soon as she did she kind of jumped forward and leant over the table, surprising me with a kiss on the cheek.

'We've been so worried about you,' she said. 'It's not like you to miss quiz night. It was–' she pulled herself backwards, her eyes locked on mine as if doubting my physical presence '–like you'd vanished off the face of the earth. Three days it's been, and not a word. No one knew where you'd gone. Holly's been beside herself. But now I've found you!' She practically squealed the last sentence.

I didn't want to think about Holly, not now.

'Come on,' she said, getting up again. 'Let's head back to the Half Moon, there's time – they'll still be there.'

'Wait,' I said. But my mind was empty, I couldn't think what to say.

'What? Oh, of course, you've got to finish your pint.'

Stealthily, and, I hoped, unnoticed, I pushed my rucksack further away, so Becki's long legs wouldn't find it.

This was what I'd always feared, being caught out at the last minute.

'We thought something terrible had happened.'

Something terrible has *happened*, I thought, *you've caught me.*

'But this is so marvellous. And you're OK?'

Her hand reached across the table, like the kiss, as if anxious to reassure herself that I was there, that I was real.

I was puzzled. Here I was, about to disappear without a word, deceiving everyone, not giving a damn, and yet on her face was nothing but pure joy at finding me. And I was betraying her, and all my friends here. She cared, they all did.

'Let's ring Holly now, tell everyone the good news.'

She placed her handbag on the table and I wondered what that crowd the other side of the bar, still frantically scribbling in their notebooks, made of this. One of them was vacantly glancing over in my direction.

Don't you dare, I said under my breath. 'Becki–'

She'd picked up her phone. 'Holly! You won't believe – yes. I found him. Yes, really. He's sitting right here.'

'Becki, let me–' I tried again.

'You'll never guess,' she carried on. 'I tried everywhere. No, of course he's not in the White Horse. That was the first place I went. The Railway Inn. Really. I don't know – I'll ask him. I just got here. He hasn't said.'

I started to motion frantically at her.

'What is it? Oh God, Holly, I'm such a twat sometimes. I'll pass him over.'

I took her phone.

'Nick!' said Holly, her voice subdued, barely above a whisper. 'What happened to you? God, I'm so relieved. I was so worried when I didn't hear from you, and no one's seen you, and then you missed quiz night, and I rang and rang and then I thought–' her voice quivered and broke. 'And you're OK?'

'Yes,' I said, trying to avoid Becki's eyes. 'I'm fine.' Holly's voice became muffled; I heard talking but couldn't make it out.

'Are you still there, Nick? It's so good to hear your voice. We'll come straight down now the quiz has finished. See you soon.'

Christ, what was I going to do? Still no trains. And now Holly and the rest of the gang were going to be here as well as Becki. Fifteen, twenty minutes at most. I might not get away.

That ticket was burning red hot in my pocket, but I didn't know what to think when I looked up and saw the sheer delight shining in Becki's eyes. And Holly's voice just now, trembling, barely this side of tears – I felt like a complete low-life.

Becki took her phone back and leant forwards.

'Aren't you going to buy me a drink now I've found you? We should definitely celebrate – it's so great knowing you're all right.'

I thought quickly. If I went to the bar there was a chance I could use the opportunity to get away – but no, it would arouse less suspicion if I brought the drinks back first. Then I could sneak off to the gents and see if there were an escape route – an open window, a fire door perhaps. And the pint I'd left behind would buy me time, assuming it wasn't too late already.

I walked to the bar like a condemned man. 'See you've got a friend come to see you off?' said the barmaid. For a moment, I had the weirdest thoughts, switching between leaving everything behind, staying, and keeping what I'd got – and something else entirely: if I did get away, did it have to be just me? Why not take Becki along? Or the barmaid? There was no reason I had to do this alone, this time. Then cold reason splashed over me like the cola filling Becki's glass. Christ, what was I thinking?

'It's good you've got some company. Could be a long wait – they say another hour or two. Don't worry,' she said, smiling, 'we don't close till midnight tonight.'

But I didn't have that long. They would all be here in a matter of minutes. I felt my feet drag as I trudged back, as if I were in chains. Becki kept her eyes firmly on me, as if now she'd found me she didn't want to let me go. She wasn't far wrong. All my instincts said: go. If I could get away. If there were trains. And I had no idea what to say, I had no idea how to explain myself to her.

*

'Well?' said Becki, when I got back from the bar. Her voice was suddenly several degrees cooler. 'What are you doing here, in this pub?'

'What do you mean?'

'Come on, Nick, sitting by yourself, missing quiz night, when you never miss it? Are you avoiding us? Is it something we've done? Has something happened? No one's heard from you, no one's seen you in days. You don't answer your phone – it goes straight to voicemail, you don't reply to texts. And as for Holly, she's been in a terrible state. Talk to me, Nick. What's this all about?'

That was the mistake I'd made. Letting quiz night become

a regular habit. Surreptitiously I glanced at my watch. Minutes were ticking past.

When I'd left other towns, it was easy. Like walking out the door, or cutting a piece of string. I disappeared, and I felt nothing. It was a clean break. But this time…. Now I'd spoken to Holly I could see her in my mind's eye, with those sad, forlorn green eyes, the ones that had captivated me, shaking her head and saying slowly the same words as Becki, only more softly. *Why, Nick? What's all this about? Is it us?* And I wouldn't be able to answer. Deep inside, I was trembling. I'd always got clean away before. But there was still time, wasn't there? I could still do it.

Becki rested her chin on her hands, elbows on the table, her eyes searching mine as if, were she to look long enough, she'd find the truth. And I was determined she wouldn't.

'So, come on, Nick, you've hardly spoken two words. Why are you hiding away here? Is it you and Holly? Is that what this is about? You can tell me, before she gets here.'

'No, it's not Holly.'

'Is it us? Something we've said or done?'

'No.'

'Well, what is it then? Are you in some kind of trouble?'

I shook my head though she wasn't far wrong. If I didn't manage to shake her and the rest of them off, I'd be trapped here, and that was trouble. But how was I going to manage it? The clock was running down.

'So why weren't you answering your phone?'

'There's something wrong with it.'

There was, sort of: I'd thrown it in the bin.

Her feet were touching my bag under the table. There was no way I could move it without her seeing.

'Come on. This is all very odd. What's really going on with you?'

I felt a cold shiver. 'Odd? What do you mean?'

'This just doesn't make sense.' A crease appeared on her forehead.

'It's like you're waiting for someone. Or something. Is that what's going on? Are you meeting someone here? Another woman? That's it, isn't it? That's the only reason I can think of. That's why you weren't speaking to any of us, isn't it? That's why you're so uncomfortable. You're planning to dump Holly, aren't you? I knew it, that's what this is all about.'

'Of course not. Don't be silly. I'm not dumping Holly. Don't be ridiculous,' I blurted out.

'Then what? This is so weird.'

'There's nothing weird about it.' I sighed heavily. 'I just needed some space. There's stuff I needed to work out.'

Frantically I tried to think. I had barely ten minutes till the rest of them arrived – could I still get away? But there was no sign of any trains running yet. What a mess this was.

'You know you can trust me,' she said. 'Talk to me.' She

reached across, a smile melted her frown and she gently caressed my hand. I couldn't help remembering last Christmas at the Half Moon, when Holly turned to me, and gently brushed her tiny hands down my back, as she said in that quiet voice of hers, 'And what do you want for Christmas, Nick?', leaning in close to give me a lingering, unexpected kiss. Suddenly, it was like the Half Moon, packed with shouted conversations and laughter, had vanished, and it was just me and her in the whole world.

But the image wouldn't hold, another replaced it, this time of Holly crying, and, try as I might, I couldn't get it out of my head. It was all my fault. I would have to live with it.

What was the matter with me? Everything was getting messy. Now I knew why I never thought about the people I left behind. If I did that, I'd never leave.

'I'm not, I dunno, I just needed to think about things, that's all,' I blurted out.

'What things? I don't understand what you mean.'

'Stuff, that's all.'

She kept pushing, and I didn't know what to do. I couldn't think. There was very little time left.

'I'm just nipping to the gents,' I told her.

Her eyes followed me to the toilet door, just like they had when I went to the bar.

Once inside the gents I found a cubicle, and I let out a relieved sigh. I locked the door and leant against it. I had to get away from Becki just so I could think, but now I only had five minutes to decide.

I'd never, ever, felt like this. I'd never felt so torn about moving on. I could – though it seemed so alien to me – feel the warmth, and the warm glow of belonging. I was surrounded by such love. I'd never had that before. For once I felt like I belonged, and I didn't deserve it. Because I don't belong. I can't belong. But was this what others had? Was this how they lived? Could I accept belonging, and forget about my need for freedom?

I was like a quantum particle, poised in an indeterminate state. Like Schrödinger's cat I was neither alive nor dead – but I had to collapse the probability wave, and become one or the other. What would they find if they burst in? Would they find me still in here, innocently washing my hands, or would I be gone?

I'd spotted the window in the gents, slightly ajar, as soon as I walked in. It was inviting. I even peered out, to see the car park and the lights of the station beyond. There was my means of escape. I wasn't stuck. I might have to leave my bag behind, but that didn't matter. There was nothing I really needed.

But still I stood, frozen, unsure what to do.

Did I go out the window – or go back through the door? Time to choose.

I chose. Taking a step, followed by a deep breath, I walked

back through the door. I chose life. I didn't know if I'd done the right thing, but on seeing Becki's anxious face I knew I had people who cared about me here. If I'd sneaked out of the window, like a burglar, what would I have had? Nothing. Now I was no longer half alive and half dead. I was alive.

I sat down at the table. Someone was playing the piano, badly, but I didn't care.

A railway worker in a hi-vis jacket barged through the door.

'Trudy, got anyone waiting for a train? There's a Bristol coming in about fifteen.'

The barmaid jerked her thumb towards me. I ignored them.

'Becki, let's go back to the Half Moon. We can meet the others on the way.'

We got up. I furtively worked the ticket out of my pocket, tossing it onto a nearby seat. As we got up and walked past, she saw it lying there.

'Look, someone's lost their ticket,' she said, bending down to pick it up.

'Plymouth – today's date too. Well, doesn't look like they're going anywhere, not without a ticket,' she said, dropping it back on the table. 'Don't forget your rucksack.'

2018

Jimmy, Eric the Panda, and Laptop John

by Grant Waters

There are two ways to access the Railway Inn: you can walk through the main entrance or go up the ramp and through the back door on your mobility scooter. Jimmy drove his with attitude, he always took the corners too fast and made people step aside. His lungs had collapsed due to years of smoking; he had reluctantly given up but nonetheless would still follow along behind a smoker to be carried along in the slipstream of their fumes.

Jimmy had walked, staggered, and tripped through the main entrance of the Inn more times than he could remember, and had even been employed as a doorman on Sundays back in the 1980s on band nights. He loved the prestige of working the door, but in the end lost the job due to 'overenthusiasm' as he called it, and they'd got some burly Yorkshireman in instead. Jimmy remained a loyal customer even now that it had been gentrified, with a coffee machine, and brunch advertised on the blackboards indoors.

For well over a hundred years the pub had sat across the

road from the railway station, but with the town redevelopment it had faced demolition. There had been a concerted effort by locals to save the pub, it was the best-known landmark in that part of town. A standoff with the bulldozers had been discussed, 'They're not going through us!' the regulars had declared.

Order was restored when it was proposed that the pub would make a great focal point for the development and give a warmth to the pedestrianised space that the other new glass and steel structures lacked. The hubbub of traffic and noise from the road was now in the past, and smart new paving had been laid across the street from the railway station concourse, right up to the edge of the pub. The Railway Inn came to resemble a proud old fighting ship that had come to rest in dry dock.

Jimmy parked just inside, got up and walked the short distance to the bar. 'Not many regulars,' he remarked, 'just a load of laptops.'

Jimmy saw it as a pub of two halves: old customers and new, or 'drinkers' and 'laptops' as he put it. The laptops used the pub as an office. 'Time was,' thought Jimmy, 'you'd come to the pub to get away from work, but this lot just drink coffee and carry on with their eyes down.' But Jimmy was in no position to preach about lifestyles, he was now a fair-weather customer: he did not, could not, venture out in the winter after dark, as the night-time air was not kind to his lungs. He never admitted this to the others, but they all suspected as much.

Eric walked in and nodded to Jimmy.

'Eric, mate,' Jimmy said, 'what are you doin' in here? Be careful now, you'll get your panda paws over everything.'

Eric was a chubby man with dark hair and bushy eyebrows. He once made the mistake of arriving at the pub wearing a padded black anorak, and immediately the comparison was made. Someone signed him up to the World Wildlife Fund for Nature just because it used a Panda as its emblem.

There was no escaping it now, he received panda birthday cards and cuddly pandas for Christmas. There were even unfair comparisons made between the difficulty in getting pandas to mate and Eric's reluctance to get the next round. Eric didn't seem to mind, he liked the attention. He even wore a WWF membership T-shirt when he played in the darts team, he said it brought him luck.

Eric approached the bar.

'Morning, Eric,' smiled the barmaid. Everyone knew Eric enjoyed passing the time of day with her, she was an attractive woman, though much too young for him.

He took his drink and walked back to Jimmy. 'You know,' said Jimmy, 'it's a wonder how you manage to hold a pint in those paws without spilling any.'

Eric began to moan about this and that: his car letting him

down just after the service, his wife wanting to spend money around the house – when all the while his kids sat around doing nothing. The list was endless.

'Is this happy hour?' enquired Jimmy.

The joke was lost on Eric, who resumed his moaning: 'How am I expected to pay for it all? – that's what I'd like to know.'

Just then a customer let out a loud exclamation: 'What the–! No, seriously that is not acceptable!' The man stared accusingly at his phone.

'Laptops are taking over this pub,' Jimmy wheezed. 'That geezer's always in here, runnin' some business, and all he drinks is skinny lattes. Shouldn't be in a pub. I'd've thrown him out when I was doorman.'

Jimmy felt very proprietorial towards his local, which made his welcoming of the new landlord three years ago, Christopher, and his partner, all the more surprising. 'Nice to have you on board,' he told him, as if he were welcoming a colleague. 'And Gabby too,' he quickly added. 'Let's hope you can make a success of things now we've been surrounded by a load of flashy shops.'

Jimmy didn't mind change, he just wanted it on his own terms: new artisan beers? Why not? Better food? It *was* about time he started being healthier, so long as the prices weren't silly. The laptops, now that was another matter: they didn't join in with the banter, they looked smug. They looked, with some justification, mused Jimmy, as if they had a better pot to piss in.

Laptop John

The chaps' conversation was disturbed when a young man began to argue with the landlord.

'I *am* over eighteen, I just don't have my ID.' He wouldn't take no for an answer, he wasn't concerned that the publican could lose his licence, he just wanted to save face in front of his friend. He raised his voice to a more threatening level and leant over the bar. 'You're embarrassing me, mate!' His eyes widened and he reached towards Christopher.

'This is like the old days,' thought Jimmy, but now he couldn't do anything, his lungs could barely get him up to the bar unaided. His chest began to tighten as he looked on helplessly. Then an intervention came from an unexpected source.

'Don't be a prick,' shouted the 'laptop', who was now standing behind the youth.

The troublemaker turned and stared at the man who had dared to confront him. He tried to work out what made him look so confident and self-assured. What would he bring to the fight? In the end, his friend dragged him away and the customary insults were called out once they were safely outside.

There was a cheer from the table as Jimmy and the boys congratulated the 'laptop' on a job well done.

'I'm getting this geezer a drink,' declared Jimmy, before Christopher told them, 'There's no need, it's on the house.' The 'laptop' smiled shyly, took his beer, nodded to the chaps at the table and resumed his work.

Jimmy was impressed. 'He done a good job,' he thought. 'In my day you just smacked 'em one.'

The next day the chaps' table was full, and they all watched as Laptop walked in. 'Could get a job as a doorman,' remarked Jimmy.

'Well, I could do with the money,' replied Laptop.

Jimmy felt himself warming towards Laptop. 'He's all right, and if he doesn't want to join in with the banter, then why should he? Even if it is coffee he's drinking, he deserves a table to himself if that's what he wants.'

That afternoon, some of the chaps wandered over and started to ask him questions. He politely answered, then he surprised them almost as much as he had the previous day: 'I'm not just here for the wifi, I'm here for the same reason as you – it's better than being at home.' He held out his hand. 'John's the name. Industrial designer.' The chaps shook his hand.

They joked about the pub getting ideas above its station now the area had been cleaned up and educated blokes like him were frequenting it. He should be on *Dragon's Den*, they told him. Then they saw that he wanted to get on. He was a busy man. He was given the nickname Laptop John, to distinguish him from John the Mechanic, who only came in occasionally and played in the darts team.

*

Laptop John was a successful designer who had his own consultancy. He was married to a beautiful woman called Caroline and they had two young daughters, Catrina and Gemma. Life seemed idyllic, although Caroline had long since got fed up letting her own career stall while his progressed. When their eldest turned four, Caroline demanded that he relinquish his study to give the girls separate rooms. He had stoically removed the maps pasted to the walls, and repapered in gender-neutral colours. Catrina now had her own space to aid personal development, and John had a smart-looking shed in the garden.

'We always put on a good show when friends visit, but, you know, there are cracks beginning to appear,' Laptop John moaned one evening after buying a round.

Disquiet had trickled into their daily lives, and then quite suddenly the trickle turned into a flood. His wife was intelligent and sharp-witted, but she turned her talents to belittling him, and now he was struggling to keep on top of his work. In the early days she had helped him, now his personal failings were mocked: *she* wouldn't have got into such a position in the first place, she would have managed her time better, and she wouldn't have gone to the pub all afternoon! When his ego was more bruised than he could bear, violent thoughts would enter his head, but the girls were always nearby, and he wasn't that sort of man.

Nearly every day now, John sought sanctuary at the Railway Inn. Jimmy began to invite him over to join the chaps, and after a drink or two John occasionally found himself telling of his marital problems.

'Oh mate,' said Jimmy, 'I got divorced twenty years ago, never looked back.'

John was then regaled with a succession of ex-wife jokes which he resisted at first, but he soon succumbed, grateful for the chance to laugh.

Jimmy was selling tickets to a local charity boxing match. 'Should be a good night,' he assured the chaps. John brought a ticket. His wife deplored violence and, right now, that seemed a very good reason to go.

*

Early on Friday evening the chaps gathered in the pub and John the Mechanic wasted no time in bringing the mood down by complaining of a downturn in business.

'Blame Brexit,' said Eric, the only one of the chaps who didn't vote for it. The table became argumentative, so Jimmy decided to lighten things up with a joke.

'Eric, does your missus ever complain about the size of

your tiny panda penis?'

Eric gave a long-suffering sigh. 'No, she's never complained about the size of it, thank you very much!'

'No,' replied Jimmy, 'she never complained about mine neither!' There was laughter around the table and one by one the others joined in.

'She was well impressed with mine!' said John the Mechanic.

'Yeah, couldn't get enough of it, and she made me breakfast.'

They turned to a tall man called George who was always a little slow at this sort of exchange. 'Err, yeah, I shagged her too!'

George had at least tried his best, but he too was now due for a bit of banter. 'Killer one-liner mate. Have you thought of doing *Live at the Apollo*?'

George nodded sarcastically then looked down at his beer, and after a while the others did the same.

A little later the silence was broken by Laptop John calling over to them, 'Eric, give me your number.'

Eric did as he was bid and soon a cartoon was sent, depicting post-coital pandas in a bed, the male with Eric written on his T-shirt. 'It's all a matter of technique', read the caption.

'That's brilliant, mate,' declared Eric. 'That's gonna be my new darts T-shirt.'

The night air was descending and Jimmy remarked that he had things to do. John said goodnight, wondering why no one questioned why Jimmy always seemed to slip away so early. John stayed until closing time, and then returned home drunk.

When John reached his front door, he found himself experiencing considerable difficulty putting the key into the lock. In the end it seemed easier to just knock. The hall light came on and Gemma started crying. The door opened and the greeting was predictable: 'You're drunk! How dare you wake the children?' He walked into the kitchen to get a drink of water and listened as Caroline marched back up the stairs. Moments later, bedding was thrown down into the hallway. Not for the first time, he slept on the sofa.

He was wrong, he admitted he was wrong, but did she have to turn the girls against him? The next morning it was, 'Oh, I know that you're tired darling, that's because Daddy was very selfish and woke you up.' Then, 'We're going to Nanna and Grandad's to stay but Daddy will be far too busy to come with us. He is always too busy, isn't he?'

After they'd left, John returned to the Railway Inn. He found the straightforwardness of the chaps to be just what he needed right now. They were not without sympathy, but they would not tolerate self-pity, and knowing that seemed to help keep him strong. He could not bring himself to confide in friends or family, as everyone else he knew thought that his was the perfect marriage.

The Boxing Match

The following Saturday, the chaps met at the football club function room. This was going to be a night of the finest white-collar boxing. Jimmy's mobility scooter guaranteed a priority position and he led the charge to the front row with the others following in his wake.

The first fight got off to a cracking start: a middleweight bout between a stocky Irishman and a taller, thinner Afro-Caribbean man. There was unanimous agreement that 'The black geezer had a very good left hand.'

As the first round ended, the ring girls stepped in. Miniskirted beauties paraded themselves while holding up numbered cards, but where were the wolf whistles of appreciation? Jimmy sat in disbelief at the polite silence from the men in the crowd who, moments earlier, had been baying for blood. This was political correctness gone mad! In the end the referee grabbed the MC's microphone and chastised the audience, 'Make some noise for these girls!' The crowd obliged and the two young women smiled mischievously.

Later, during the interval, Jimmy remembered a job that wanted doing and said that he had seen the best fight of the night already.

'Stay to the end, I'll drive you home,' said John. 'I can fit your wheels in my people carrier.'

Around midnight they went to the carpark and Jimmy found himself impressed as John lifted his scooter into the back of the people carrier with comparative ease.

John asked for Jimmy's postcode and set the sat nav for an estate on the edge of town. On the drive, a radio station played in the background that Jimmy was unfamiliar with. He found himself momentarily attempting to follow an analysis on what a post-Brexit economy would look like. He soon gave up.

'How is it with the missus?' he enquired.

'Not good, not good at all, she's at her parents' and won't let me see the girls.'

Jimmy shook his head and let out a low hissing sound between his teeth. 'Been there, mate, been there.'

There followed a long silence that was broken when John remarked, 'I used to drive an F-Type Coupé, but I sold it when the kids came along. I missed it at first but then the kids just sort of took over.'

'Well, now you can go back to it,' Jimmy responded helpfully. 'Get another car, mate, get another girl. Move on, it's the only way.'

John snorted faintly. He wasn't ready to hear this sort of advice just yet, it sounded too brutal, too final.

They talked about the evening's fights and then Jimmy

mentioned the disappointing response of the crowd towards the ring girls. 'It was a poor show; they deserved better.'

John nodded. 'Men don't seem to know what to do these days. I suppose it was more straightforward in your day....' He trailed off, and found his mind drifting as they got closer to their destination.

Dark thoughts entered John's head. He reflected on his own girls and their futures: would he still be in their lives? What if they ever wanted to dress like ring girls: would his advice still count? If it came to it, he hoped Caroline wouldn't move them too far away. He considered other scenarios and they all seemed unbearable.

They arrived at a small terraced house on an estate that looked like it needed as much regeneration as the town centre had recently received. John turned to Jimmy, 'You know, I used to play darts with my father when I was a kid, I got quite good. Maybe I should join the team?'

Jimmy sucked in air slowly, 'Yeah, do that, mate.'

2019

We'll Meet Again

by Sheila Davie

'Not seen 'im before,' Joel muttered as he watched a middle-aged man stoop to enter the bar. Thursday nights were generally quiet, especially at this time of year, when the number of tourists had dwindled, when the locals could have a bit of peace and reminisce about the good old days.

The landlord was out at a meeting and had left the barman, Karl, in charge, with the help of the latest barmaid, a brunette in her forties, who didn't seem to know her ass from her elbow when it came to beer and ale.

The stranger nodded a greeting and began taking stock of his surroundings, looking across at the board listing tonight's specials and the screen showing the train times. Joel watched. He observed the stranger approach the piano, lift the lid, stroke the keys, and sit down on the stool. The first haunting chords of 'We'll Meet Again' resonated around the room and struck the pit of Joel's stomach. Joel wanted him to stop playing but, when he opened his mouth to shout, nothing but beer froth spewed out.

'What's up, Joel, mate?' Karl asked, pulling his usual pint. 'You look as if you've seen a ghost.'

Joel tried to compose himself. What was happening?

There had been a few strange events in the pub lately: doors open that should have been locked, voices upstairs when he'd just been told the bedrooms were empty, that sort of thing. And now, all of a sudden, that song again. He knew he had to be careful.

'Leave it out, you're doing my 'ead in,' he called across the room. The stranger looked up and struck several more keys in spite of Joel's protest. Joel's heart was beating fast now, in tandem with the little hammers inside the piano vibrating the strings. The stranger paused, cast what Joel thought was a meaningful look, a smirk, before the lid went down like a coffin top on the keys.

The stranger came up to the bar and ordered a cold beer. 'Better make that a lager, please,' he corrected himself.

Joel detected a slight American accent. He thought the man might be of a similar age to his son, give or take a year or two, and with the same sandy-coloured hair.

'Hope I didn't upset you there, buddy,' he said to Joel as he settled onto the adjacent stool. 'It's such a lovely song and my Grandpa used to play it. He was over here, you know, in the war. In this actual place.'

Joel relaxed and allowed himself a smile.

'It's OK,' he said, 'it's just that my mother passed away recently and we had that song at her funeral. She lived nearby all her life.' The man nodded his condolences, and Joel went on, thinking aloud. 'I wonder if they ever met?

She often talked about dances in the function room behind the pub, where the Tommies were jealous of the handsome GIs – thought they would take their girls off to the USA I suppose.'

Joel was on a roll now, but kept his voice low so he couldn't be overheard.

'That piano's been here since the war, you know. Seen lots of action and could tell a tale or two.' He winked conspiratorially.

'So, you lived here long, Joel? Can I call you Joel?' The stranger looked over at the barman. He must have overheard Karl saying his name.

'I left years ago and only came back when Mum became ill. Now she's left me the house, I thought I might as well stay. I do miss the Spanish sunshine though, and the expat lifestyle. I used to pop over to see Mum a couple of times a year and visit some old mates who live in London.'

The barmaid was earwigging from next to the till. She came over and chipped in, 'Yeah, Joel's told me about some of his escapades – tell him about the time you came back for your fiftieth birthday.'

Joel cringed inwardly. He'd drunk a bit too much the other night and told her a lot of stories. But this one was a good story. 'June 1994, stayed with a mate in Tottenham. Awesome.' Then he stopped in his tracks as he realised his mistake: he'd mentioned Tottenham. Too late to cover it up, and now the barmaid was heading for the piano.

'Did you know, Joel,' said the stranger, sitting up straighter, 'your old mate from Tottenham has been telling tales about you. He did time for a jewellery heist, whereas some of the gang, naming no names, got away. It was only at your mother's funeral, hearing "We'll Meet Again", and seeing you swaggering around, that he decided it was payback time.'

The barmaid lifted the piano lid and whipped out a pair of nitrile gloves and a bottle opener from her pocket. It didn't take long to locate the group of wonky keys. She teased out a tuneless chord before reaching into the piano.

A small crowd was gathering, watching the scene unfold. This was turning into another strange evening at the Railway Inn. But then, after recent events at the pub – strangers in suits coming and going without ordering anything, interference with the television signal – anything could happen.

Joel began to sweat. Was he hallucinating? The stranger on the barstool looked remarkably like his son. What was it his mother used to say? 'What goes around comes around.'

In the corner of the room the piano was revealing its secrets: an old postcard, folded, with the message 'We'll Meet Again', and taped to the back a small brown envelope. The barmaid shook the contents into her hand. The crowd parted as she tipped the haul of tiny diamonds back in the envelope and returned to the bar. When she pulled out a warrant card the silence was palpable.

'Joel Donald Jordan, I'm arresting you on suspicion of robbery. You do not have to say anything, but it may harm your defence if you do not mention when questioned something which you later rely on in court. Anything you do say may be given in evidence.'

He knew the game was up. He'd been careless, let something slip after a few too many drinks. The bitch would have his fingerprints from a glass: they'd have proof he'd been there, in Tottenham in 1994.

He was led out to an unmarked police car waiting in the car park. A few minutes later, as it pulled away, he caught the driver's mocking eyes in the rear view mirror and winced. Next to him, the undercover officer-turned-barmaid hummed that tune.

*

Driving back from his meeting, just down the road from the pub, Christopher, the landlord, saw someone slumped in the hedgerow. Another drunk, he thought. Pulling up, he realised whoever it was had been beaten up. It was a middle aged man with sandy hair. The man groaned.

'I'll call the police,' Christopher said. 'And an ambulance.'

'I am the police,' said the beaten-up man. 'But make that call anyway.'

Christopher offered the man his hand to help him stand.

'Grandpa Don always said this was an interesting place,' the man moaned as the landlord pulled him to his feet. 'In more ways than one.'

Spirit Hunters

by Sarah Byrne

'It was on a cold November night, under the light of a full moon, when, for one young woman, the Railway Inn turned into a house… of murder.'

'Isn't this all a bit much?' Bill, the camera guy mumbled to himself. Clara put down her script and tutted at him. 'It's a little Hammer Horror already with all of this.' He waved a dismissive hand at the revellers garbed in Victorian dress in the bar. There were at least five Jack the Rippers and a gaggle of bloodied prostitutes, as well as a couple of Sherlock Holmeses and one disgruntled young woman who appeared to be the sole attendee in accurate period dress.

'Are you kidding? This is amazing!' Clara tossed her hair behind her shoulders in preparation for the first take. She finally seemed happy with her opening monologue. Perhaps now they could actually start filming? 'We're celebrating the heritage of this place. Ooh, Gabby, over here!' A smartly dressed blonde woman materialised behind the bar and met Clara with a squeal that descended into peals of laughter and gushing declarations that this place was the *absolute best* and that Gabby was such a *darling* letting them film in her pub and so on and so on. The first take would have to wait.

Bill turned his attention to Felicity, the production assistant, and rolled his eyes.

'I think she forgets sometimes this is peak trash TV.'

Felicity suppressed a snort of laughter, eyes darting over to Clara, who was too preoccupied with her old friend to notice.

'Some people really believe in this stuff though,' she said.

'Please don't tell me you're one of them,' Bill scoffed as he fiddled with the camera.

'Not really.' Felicity shuffled a little on the spot. 'But you know they filmed an episode of *Haunted Hotel* here in the mid-2000s? That's why Clara asked her friend if we could come here in the first place. Besides, a place as old as this has a kind of presence about it, right?'

'Yeah, tacky gastro pub pretending to be chic,' said Bill. 'Stand there for a sec, I want to adjust the lens.'

'Someone did die here though,' Felicity persevered, trying to get Bill to be less cynical. Moving in front of the camera, Felicity took a moment to look around the room. Tacky wasn't the word she'd have used, though it did look like it was going for two competing aesthetics, half cosy and welcoming and half chic and sophisticated. Neither had really won but there was a charm to it. Bill was used to drinking in places with living walls, experimental open mic nights, and where the food was served on things that weren't plates.

'People die everywhere,' Bill said. 'With all the people who have ever lived it's just basic statistics that wherever you are at any given moment someone died on that exact spot.'

'But we know that she died in one of the bedrooms upstairs.' Felicity's voice dropped to a whisper. 'Didn't you read the old police records?'

He looked at her like she'd suggested he eat some puppies. This wasn't a job you did for ideological reasons.

'If you lot are ready to do your jobs,' – Clara strode back to them – 'let's try another take. We're on a schedule. Where's Lewis? Shouldn't the producer be producing this show?'

'Chatting to the owner in the office upstairs, trying to work out where we're putting the gear later,' said Bill.

Clara made a sound halfway between a groan and a wail. Felicity half expected her to stamp her foot.

'Fine. I'll grab him when he comes down. Roll the camera.'

Immediately the scowl turned to a megawatt smile as Clara addressed the camera.

'Welcome to *Spirit Hunters*, I'm Clara McKenzie and tonight we're at the Railway Inn, a beautifully refurbished pub that hides a dark secret. A century and a half ago, this was a refuge for weary travellers to rest on long journeys, and it remained that way as the railways cut through the beautiful countryside. People from all walks of life and with all kinds of motivations stayed within these walls looking for peace and rest – until the unthinkable happened. It was on a cold November night, under the light of a full moon, when, for one young woman, the Railway Inn turned into a house… of murder.'

The entire room plunged into darkness and a strangled cry was heard. It was shortly followed by a shout of 'Sorry, tripped the fuse!' and 'That was my drink!'

A second later the lights sputtered back on and the barman, Karl, began furiously apologising to one of the prostitutes.

'Want to go again?' Bill asked Clara.

*

'What's with the costumes?' Felicity asked Lewis later that evening, as Bill was setting up a shot of Clara behind the bar. Gabby's husband, Christopher, was enthusiastically telling her how they had renovated the inn when they bought the freehold a few years ago, while Clara nodded and swiped through her phone.

'It's the anniversary of the murder,' Lewis explained, 'so Chris and Gabby thought it would bring in customers. They've done a couple of ghost walks around the local area that went down well. Depravity sells.'

'You don't approve?'

'I produce a ghost-hunting show whose main audience is crackpots and stoned students. I don't get to judge. Can you go and tell Eliza it's nearly time? We'll do the piece with Clara and Chris, and then film Eliza "sensing" whatever it is.'

'Are we really going to stay the whole night?'

'Not a chance. Eliza and Clara can do their séance skit and we'll set up the spirit box and the infrasound sensor, and by midnight we'll be done.'

'What if we find something though?' Felicity asked.

The only response was a withering look.

*

'As always, I'm joined by world-renowned paranormal investigator and psychic, Eliza Bay. Eliza, what are your first impressions of the Railway Inn?'

'Well the food here is delicious and don't get me started on the gin,' Eliza laughed. 'There was a warm, welcoming presence when we first arrived. This building has a caring nature; it wants to nurture the patrons.'

'Good grief,' Lewis muttered under his breath. Gabby and Chris meanwhile were beaming off-camera. They had taken care to make the place suitably atmospheric for their special guests, chalking up NO LAPTOPS TONIGHT on one of the boards, and covering the TV with a cheap oil painting Chris had found in the attic.

'Underneath that, however,' Eliza continued, 'there is

something darker. A sadness permeates this place, regret, sorrow, desperation, fear.'

'Make a note to cut some of that,' murmured Lewis.

'What do you mean?' Clara asked Eliza. She tilted her head to the side and pouted slightly. This, her trademark expression, was supposed to indicate a deep interest or passion, but Lewis thought it just made her look like she had an upset stomach.

'Something terrible happened here,' Eliza said. 'One hundred and twenty-five years ago this very night, a young woman met her end, and her spirit remains here. She's unable to move on because of the trauma of her death.

'And tonight, viewers, we are going to attempt to contact her. Margaret Johnson was just twenty-one when she was stabbed to death in a bedroom here at the Railway Inn. Fleeing an arranged marriage, Margaret sought refuge here and only found death when her fiancé caught up with her. With the kind permission of the Railway Inn's owners, we have set up state-of-the-art detection equipment in the room where the murder took place, as well as in the hallway outside, and in the main eating area we're in now. In addition, Eliza will attempt to psychically contact Margaret's spirit and discern why she hasn't moved on.'

'Cut!' yelled Lewis. He turned to Felicity who was scribbling notes on the shot list. 'Maybe Margaret likes the gin selection too?' he muttered, rolling his eyes.

'Maybe she's waiting here to exact revenge for her murder!' Felicity was practically jumping up and down with excitement.

'I'm not even going to dignify that with a response,' said Lewis. 'Can you go check the cameras upstairs are streaming?'

The refurbishment upstairs was thorough, and beautifully executed. The walls featured glossy paper and the old floorboards creaked under the plush carpet. But at the far end of the hall, one of the light bulbs was on the blink, bathing the corridor in an eerie flicker.

'You're with those people aren't you?'

Felicity responded with a strangled cry that died in her throat as she whipped around, coming face to face with the girl in the Victorian dress she'd seen downstairs.

'I came up here for a bit of peace and quiet,' she continued, fiddling with her hands.

Close up, the costume was even more impressive. A lot of time and effort had gone into it. The stitching was neat, and there were even signs of wear and mending as if this was a real garment that had been worn day in day out rather than a replica. She must be one of those professional re-enactors, Felicity decided. Gabby and Chris were known for pulling out all the stops for events.

'I, uh, yeah,' Felicity attempted to claw back some dignity after her scream. 'Sorry, I didn't expect anyone to be up here. I'm Felicity.'

'I'm Peggy.' She gave a small half-smile. 'I hope you don't mind the company. It's too noisy and crowded downstairs.'

'You're not here for the party?' Felicity frowned. 'Do you work here?'

'Kind of,' said the girl. So, definitely a re-enactor then. 'What are you doing?'

'Checking the cameras to make sure they're recording. You know, for when the ghost turns up.'

It was meant as a joke but Peggy's lip curled and she looked away.

'People here are obsessed with that ghost story. Like it's a joke or publicity or something.'

'It's dumb, I know.' Felicity's shoulders sagged. 'We never get any proof on camera, but the audience likes it.'

Suddenly serious, Peggy said, 'People seem to like focusing on others' pain as entertainment. They're constantly either reading about horrific things on their phones or watching some awful true crime documentary, or reading trashy murder mystery novels.'

Felicity gaped at her, trying to think of something to say. 'Do you want to see the set up?' was what she settled on. This earned her a look halfway between arrogance and intrigue. It was like Peggy was studying some unusual insect.

'I don't know a lot about making a television programme,'

Peggy said, tilting her head to one side. 'It might be interesting.'

'It is!' Felicity said. She bounded into one of the bedrooms and gestured at the rig of cameras dotted around. 'Lewis – he's the producer – wants every angle covered. The cameras are transmitting to the van outside that has our sound and vision mixers in.'

'What does that mean?'

'Sound and vision mixers are people who edit the content. So they take the raw footage from the cameras, cut it up and sort out the order of the shots.'

'I see. And what are these other machines?'

'Eliza brought these.'

'Oh.' Peggy's voice dripped with contempt. 'The psychic.'

'That's her.' Felicity tried not to wince at the word 'psychic'. 'I don't know a lot about these, but that over there is a spirit box. It's a kind of radio and it scans frequencies that people believe ghosts communicate on.'

'That's ridiculous. What else is there?'

'Um, in the next room there are instruments for registering temperature, a Geiger counter–'

'A what?'

'A Geiger counter. It measures changes in radiation. There's also an EMF meter. Electro-magnetic frequency?'

Peggy looked at Felicity blankly and then turned away. When said out loud it did kind of sound like nonsense.

'Do any of you actually believe in ghosts?' Peggy asked.

'Eliza obviously does. I'm not sure about Clara, our presenter. The crew definitely don't, Lewis especially – he says it's stupid all the time.'

'And you?'

Felicity hesitated, her face growing hot.

'I don't *not* believe.' She dragged the words out slowly.

'Is that why you're here?' Peggy smirked. 'You want to meet a ghost?'

Felicity shifted from side to side. Actually yes, that was why she was here. It was the whole reason she'd applied for a job on this show in the first place. It wasn't like she was interested in a career in TV; she wanted a chance to see more, to experience the unknown.

'Why?' Peggy asked. 'I mean why do you want to meet a ghost?'

'I guess to know that there's something else out there,' said Felicity. She waved an arm around the room. 'Something after all of this.'

'I see,' Peggy nodded. 'You want something – a ghost – to tell you that there is meaning to life. That it isn't all for nothing.'

'I guess.'

'Be careful what you wish for,' Peggy smiled. 'Perhaps tonight will be your lucky night.'

Before Felicity could respond, Peggy was out the door.

She must have moved fast because by the time Felicity stuck her head out the hallway was empty. Her stomach twisted.

'All good?' Lewis appeared at the top of the stairs.

'Yeah, everything's working.'

'Great. Let's get this ridiculous show on the road.'

*

'Is that… whispering?'

The group crowded around the spirit box looked at each other in disbelief. Usually the spirit box produced nothing but static. Some people tried to warp the incoherent sounds into muffled words, but Felicity was pretty sure no one had ever picked up anything so clear on the device before.

Go away and leave me alone.

Go away and leave me alone.

Go away and leave me alone.

'I don't think this is possible,' frowned Clara. The speaker buzzed and crackled and there was a sound like something hard being hit. Possibly in frustration.

'It must be a radio signal the box is picking up by accident,' said Lewis. 'Maybe we could use it anyway?'

'What? Tell the audience that we recorded a ghost taking a nap? That's lazy work even for us,' said Bill.

'Well, situations like this really do require an expertise beyond the layman.' Eliza stepped back, a smug look on her face. Beside her, Felicity felt Clara tense up. 'You tinker with your little machines, I'll go and do a reading of the room.'

Eliza marched off, followed by Clara, who tried to sprint after her but was somewhat hampered by her high heels.

'She does know we don't actually care, right?' sighed Bill. 'I just want to go home.'

'We need the readings from the machines too,' said Lewis. 'It's fine, we'll make do with… whatever the hell this is. Let Eliza do her stupid reading, and then we'll make it look good in the edit. If we're lucky we can be done in a few hours.'

*

'This is the bedroom Margaret died in.' Eliza flung her arms open wide. 'There is a strong negative energy here.'

'The temperature is lower in here than anywhere else in the building,' said Clara. 'Our instruments–'

'Confirm what I just told you.'

'Yes and–'

'We are not alone,' Eliza trilled. 'Margaret, can you hear me?'

There was dead silence. Eliza's brow furrowed and her fingers flexed. She began to stride around the room, arms still raised. 'Margaret. We mean you no harm.'

Clara's hands were balled into fists and the rictus grin on her face looked in danger of slipping off at any moment. If there wasn't a ghost in here already, Felicity thought, there may be one by the time they were done, given how Clara could be when her temper got the better of her.

Minutes felt like hours. Usually Eliza would get something as soon as she walked into a room, but now there was nothing, and she was walking faster and faster, round in circles, looking increasingly distressed.

'What do we do?' Felicity mouthed at Lewis. He shrugged and looked over at Eliza with a mixture of horror and bemusement. A sour, sick feeling was beginning to build in Felicity's stomach, like something had gone terribly wrong and it was somehow her fault.

'Something wrong, Eliza?' Clara asked through gritted teeth.

'She's here! I can feel her, she's here, but… it's like she's ignoring me! Don't you dare laugh!' she shrieked, an accusing finger pointed straight at Bill.

'OK, that's enough,' Lewis said. 'Eliza do you want to take a minute?'

'I am a professional! What I need is for whichever one of you is putting out all this negative energy and blocking Margaret's signals to stop. Right now!' Felicity shrunk under Eliza's glare.

'Eliza, no one is blocking your signals. I'm calling it, we're going to take a five minute break and–'

'The door is locked, Lewis!' Felicity rattled the handle. She pounded on the door. 'This isn't funny. Let us out!'

'OK, calm down,' snapped Lewis. He pushed Felicity

aside and went to try the door. It didn't open with a simple tug so he put his full weight into it – but it wouldn't budge. Now he was angry too. 'If this is someone's stupid idea of a joke I swear to God–'

'It isn't,' Clara whispered, 'these doors only lock from the inside.'

The silence was heavy and sickening; the temperature dropped suddenly.

'Call Gabby or Chris,' Lewis said. 'Clara! Do it!'

There was a thud as Clara's phone slipped from her shaking fingers in her rush to call for help. At the exact same moment the lights flickered, causing everyone to freeze immediately. They flickered a few more times before the room was plunged into darkness, a whimper coming from somewhere Felicity couldn't place.

'Everyone keep calm,' said Lewis though his voice was wavering. 'Clara, do you have your phone? Clara?'

There was no answer.

'Oh God, we're all going to die,' hissed Bill. 'This is–'

The lights popped back on. Everything was as it should be except that everyone was either curled in the foetal position or huddling against the wall. Lewis tried the door again and it opened with a soft click.

A sour, metallic taste filled Felicity's mouth and every muscle in her body quivered. With an obvious lack of grace she clambered to her feet, the sting in her legs receding as she shook them out.

'Everything's fine,' said Clara, though it sounded more like she was reassuring herself than them. With a beaming smile she turned back towards the camera, smoothing down her jacket. 'OK, if you've all finished playing around–'

The window flew open and a strong blast of ice-cold wind left Clara sprawled on the ground. The wind continuing to rage, Bill staggered over to try and close the window, leaning on it with all of his considerable weight. When the wind dropped abruptly he slammed it shut. In the sudden quiet Lewis tried to pull Clara to her feet – but was swiped at for his troubles.

'This is a £300 jacket,' she screeched. 'Get your greasy hands off me!'

Felicity could have sworn she'd heard a harsh laugh mixed in with the howl of the wind. The hairs on the back of her neck stood up and the feeling of being watched swept over her.

'I'm out.' Bill clutched his chest as he leaned on the window frame. 'I mean it. This place is haunted and I'm not staying here another second.'

'Everywhere we go is haunted,' said Felicity. Her voice was barely a whisper. 'This place is just more... loud about it.'

'Nowhere we visit is haunted,' Lewis hissed. 'There's no such thing as ghosts or anything like that. This place is just old. They obviously didn't do as good a job on the renovation as they led us to believe – they need to fix the doors and windows.'

'Chris and Gabby are good people,' Clara wailed. 'This beautiful building was not a rush job. This is one of you.' She jabbed a finger towards Bill and Felicity. 'You're all jealous of my success and you're trying to sabotage me.'

'Success? Please! Only about twelve people watch this show and eight of them are my family members,' Bill scoffed. An animalistic cry escaped Clara as she lunged for him. But Bill was quicker on his feet, and managed to leap to the side so that Clara lost her balance and fell onto her knees.

'This is ridiculous,' Bill said. 'We need to take ten minutes and all calm down. I'm not staying here anymore. Eliza, you need to do your reading so we can all go. Eliza?'

The psychic was perched on the edge of the bed, her eyes glossy and unfocused like she was staring at something far away.

'Eliza?' Lewis' hand hovered hesitantly near her shoulder. 'Eliza are you OK?'

Eliza narrowed her eyes and straightened like some unseen force had pulled her upwards.

'Having fun?' she snapped. It didn't sound like Eliza's voice. It was colder and clipped. Bile rose in Felicity's throat and Clara let out a whimper, scrambling back towards where Felicity was cowering. 'Eliza, I know you're mad about the negative energy or whatever,' Lewis said. 'We're all having a difficult night but–'

'Oh, you have no idea what difficult is.' Eliza glared up at him. 'You come here with your boxes and your machines and your cheap, music hall clairvoyant, and you play around with things you cannot hope to understand.'

Eliza rose from the bed and Lewis took a step back, arms spread wide like he was trying to protect Clara and Felicity behind him.

'You are all poor excuses for spirit hunters,' Eliza laughed in her new voice. 'A little wind, a little darkness, and you're cowering like frightened animals.'

'Eliza, this isn't funny anymore,' Lewis warned.

'It was never funny,' Eliza yelled, and everyone flinched.

Felicity covered her mouth with her hand to muffle her sobs. Her heart was racing.

'You people take tragedy and horror and you turn it into entertainment. It's like bear-baiting or a public hanging. People watch because it's happening to someone else.' The lights began to flicker, the shadows in the lines of Eliza's face made her look demonic. 'You should all go and leave the dead in peace.'

Clara let out a cry and Lewis made a movement like he was about to run. In that very moment the flickering stopped and in the moments that followed, while they all waited in trepidation, the all-pervading cold was replaced with the warmth of before. Felicity's heart was still slamming against her ribs but the feeling of being watched was gone and the goose bumps on her skin had faded so that all that was left was a cold sheen of sweat.

'What are you staring at, Lewis?' Eliza croaked, in her own voice again. 'Why are you all... crying?' She sounded confused.

Bill was gone without bothering to answer, and all she got from Clara was retching. Lewis yanked Felicity to her feet without a word and pulled her from the room.

'What was that?' she stuttered.

'The last episode we are ever going to make,' Lewis said.

*

They sat in the bar downstairs in silence while the party atmosphere raged around them. Bill had finished his third whisky, and buried his face in his arms on the table while he muttered incoherently to himself. Felicity watched as a confused Chris and Gabby listened to Clara's wailing.

'Are they really going to cancel the show?' Felicity asked.

'Lewis seemed pretty set on it,' Bill slurred. 'At the very least he isn't coming back. And neither am I.'

'Yeah, me neither,' Felicity said. So much for her grand ghost-hunting adventure, she thought.

'OK, guys, time to go.' Lewis appeared beside them. 'I've called head office and luckily someone was still there, but...'

'What?' Bill lifted his head.

'They say it's going to make great television. They want to make an event out of it. The marketing team is already working on it.'

Felicity listened, open-mouthed. She remembered something that Peggy had said earlier: *People seem to like focusing on others' pain as entertainment.* Felicity hadn't realised the truth of it until this moment. Maybe there was still time to find her and apologise?

The team struggled to their feet in silence. Felicity didn't know why none of them was getting angry over this – over the marketing team celebrating their horror and making it into a special event; it was almost like they expected this reaction. Chris and Gabby led Clara over to join the others. The expression on their faces was an odd mixture of apology and excitement. Of course, they loved the idea of their pub being haunted.

'I'm sorry you guys were spooked,' Chris said. He followed them outside into the cold night and watched as they clambered into the van.

'Oh, hey,' Felicity stuck her head out of the window. 'Before I go, can you tell Peggy I'm sorry. I think I was kind of rude earlier.'

'Sorry, who?'

'The girl in the Victorian dress.'

'Lots of girls in Victorian dress here tonight,' Chris smiled apologetically. 'Can you be more specific?'

'The re-enactor.'

Chris frowned. 'We didn't hire anyone, and none of our staff dressed up. You sure she wasn't a customer?'

Felicity's throat tightened and a sensation similar to the one she felt in the bedroom earlier rippled across her skin.

'My mistake,' she said, and settled back in her seat, willing her heart to slow down.

Glancing up at the inn as they drove away, Felicity was sure she could make out a figure at the bedroom window.

A Portrait of a Young Woman at the Railway Inn

by Vanessa Waltz

The young woman wonders what she is doing with her life. Honestly, she sometimes swears that she can hear the crickets chirp.

The young woman considers this as she studies the menu at a cosy station pub. Next to her is the heft of an old piano, and all around is the odd aroma of alcohol. The place buzzes with robust energy. A blackboard proclaims 'Passionate about food? Try our new autumn menu!' while another announces 'Write Club: What will you write? Crime, Romance, Fantasy – Railway Inn Writers, 7pm Tonight!' A patchwork of coats passes by her in pops of colour. The mainstays of autumn dressing arrest her attention: the caps, the cardigans, the scarves jutting out just so.

The young woman has been to this pub before. On this occasion, she finds herself in unusual circumstances, or those to which she attaches unusual significance. After all, she is the sort of young woman who remembers certain things said on late, lazy, hazy afternoons – windy, *windy* afternoons – as accompanied by the squeaky peal of older pub-piano keys. She is, then, the sort of young woman who attaches certain meanings to things.

And what are these things? She opens up her journal and begins to write, in order to consider them properly.

Money is one of them. It is a concern, niggling and constant. The young woman wonders, as her eyes flick idly over the menu, if she will ever be at a point where it won't be. What would that look like? (In so wondering, she debates the financial merits of real ale. The couple running the pub have won awards for their beer, or so the sign says. Maybe she should give it a go?)

The young woman has held down a series of long-term temporary jobs. She has been, in succession, an administration assistant, administration coordinator, data entry assistant, and data entry coordinator. She is grateful for the work and enjoys it, at any rate – sometimes at any pay rate. (Here she frowns, remembering roles past.)

The young woman thinks of her present workplace, to which she will return after lunch. In the midst of entering a string of numbers into the computer, she will hear the coffee burbling delightfully away at its station; she will hear the rain pattering outside; she will stroll company paths in less rainy weather – sometimes with a colleague, sometimes by herself. In these moments, she will catch herself wondering: is she meant to be doing something else? Is there an elusive something else over which she is meant to ache, sweetly and sadly?

The young woman concludes that she has enough money for the moment. Of course, she does not have enough to put down roots in the form of purchasing a place outright. Still, she has enough to keep up with monthly payments on her comfortably cramped flat, to fix the faulty heel on a somewhat expensive shoe, to attend an orchestral performance, and to treat a few friends to drinks at this particular pub post-performance.

Other ideas and influences call to her. The young woman has interests. She dabbles in things; she attends classes. Opportunities have arisen. She is pleased by them. The young woman has the sober realisation that her line of long-term temporary work offers a sort of financial security to her, holds it out. However, the chance to advance a modest career in the arts is such that she may need to relinquish some of the paying hours of her present position in order to give herself the time to pursue said opportunities.

The young woman sips at her ale. Grumpy Railwayman, it's called: a dark colour, tasting bitter but not unpleasant. She knows that this could conceivably be what she yearns for: the exchanging of a not-so-creative life for a creative one. A small, comfortably cramped life for a larger and more uncertain one. For she has come to rely too much on the allure of the long-term temporary position: 'I can leave this work at any time' has turned into 'I am afraid to leave this work now the time has come'.

There is always romance, the young woman considers. Is her yearning in that direction? As regards men, she's not had much luck with them thus far in her fretful existence. She evaluates this state of things as she sips her aforementioned ale, its depths pooling. There has been a young man or two. There has been a pick of flowers offered to her a time or two. And what's come of it? A few doorstep kisses. A few late nights. A few somethings literally shouted in her ear as she leans forward in her seat at a jazz club. Romance, with its inelegant care – romance, or love – has found her too often slumped in front of the mirror, brooding over one too many would-be encounters.

Love is the trouble with her, the young woman thinks – she watches it walk right by.

By turns, there have been a few instances of note, a few lovely ones. If she *had* been in love once or twice, wouldn't a rush of feeling accompany her, then and now? And yet, here she is, considering the same feeling and pushing past it.

The thing is, the young woman can commit, cheerfully, to having her hand held at opportune moments, to a glass of something, to a long walk. But she does not know that she can commit to these things with one person for life, or with cheer.

'I would rather be alone,' she muses to herself, sweetly, sadly, and with quiet assurance as she sips her ale again. (Not bad, that.)

The young woman's eyes rest on the elderly men seated at the bar, their caps folded in front of them. This lot looks familiar. She might have seen them this time last week, or this time last year.

The young woman orders her lunch. It's an order pleasing in its familiarity – sandwich and side salad, please. The ale acts as a complement today; gin or apple cider could do the job credibly next week. They don't mind her drinking at lunchtime, her coworkers; it doesn't affect her work. In fact, they may not even know.

The young woman returns to her thoughts. She comes from a happy home – happy enough, the young woman corrects herself with a contemplative sip – and yet, to a degree, she likes her life the way it is. She would rather allow time for sorting out her peccadilloes, her preoccupations and even her to-dos for herself. (Time in brick-built pubs not entirely unlike this one is a help.)

There is always travel, the young woman considers. When her mind ranges over destinations, it becomes a different matter altogether. Family trips taken in her youth were bustling, colourful affairs, and an exercise in patience for all involved. Looking back, could she recall anything of interest in them? Anything of much good that came out of them?

Then there were weekend travels with friends from university: the Saturday mornings marked with anticipation of a day out, the conversations (usually of a pleasant nature), the hikes to see a particular point by the afternoon, the recommended watering holes, doubtless *the* last word in what's-to-eat-or-drink, and the least expensive bottle of wine, often of correspondingly woeful taste. The young woman recalls the at-night conversations that only left her wanting more from herself, for herself, and the resolutions accompanying Sunday evenings.

The young woman has tried to travel a bit as a young adult – with family, with friends, *once* with a young man, and at least once on her own. (She does not classify her forty-five-minute commute as 'travel'.)

The young woman sits back and considers. There is always, in her dreams, the city. It is a city not quite identifiable in its shape and scope. In spite of that, she knows at once that this place exists, and can only exist to her in this way until she encounters it in reality for the first time. It is not like those cities to which she has been. Or is it? It is a city of pep and verve, pomp and unusual circumstance.

Inwardly, the young woman wanders these city streets, observing the buzz and pattern of metropolitan life. She wanders the streets of the place in which she lives now, yes;

she often ends up in the corner in which she currently resides, kitschy mug in hand, scarf attractively arranged. Though the thought of performing these or similar actions in her city of dreaming spires lends a certain luminescence to the image.

In her dreams, the young woman breezes into a city hotel and breathlessly sets down her bags in its lobby – tea, please. The waiter knows just what to bring. Some days, it is standard English Breakfast, other days Earl Grey. Settled conspicuously into a chair, she checks her watch and thoughtfully stirs her tea, observing the balance of life before her. The lobby, wreathed with soft tones and chandeliers, oozes personality. The young woman rifles through paper selections on offer. It matters little what papers are present, only that they *are* present. She sighs happily.

The young woman thinks that she would find metropolitan life exceedingly sweet. In her dream city, she is at peace with time and place, and with herself. She finishes her tea and wanders out of the hotel lobby, out of other hotel lobbies, out of shops and parks. As to the last, yes, there are certain university parks that she likes to visit in her citified dreams. On autumn days, leaves skitter by her along the park roads; she gabbles to them internally in return.

The young woman's lunch is brought to her table, and she

is brought back to reality. Here she sits, in this station pub, with her dreams that are not *now*. With fresh resolve, she returns to her mental list of *things* as she tucks into her sandwich. A list of things that add *purposefulness* to her life.

The young woman takes walks. These walks mete out a daily form of exercise, carefully considered: thirty-three minutes in poor weather, sixty-six minutes on more forgiving days. On these walks, she pursues routes selected for a pleasing variety of reasons. One route offers a long, low, lovely stretch of houses. Another offers colourful characters. Another offers an off-kilter bookshop, its titles waving at her in breezy weather. On a good day, she is lucky enough to catch all characteristics in one well-timed walk.

The young woman performs errands. The majority of these tend to take place on weekday evenings. She feels a sense of industry here. On one evening, she can be found replacing watch batteries; on another, she returns the loafers that *do* pinch her feet, on second thoughts. On these evenings, she roams shopping centres and takes in seasonal displays. She gets her hair cut.

In each of these errands, the young woman seeks transcendence. She looks for some all-important meaning when in this frame of mind – say, when she overhears a snatch of music as she navigates her lonely local shopping centre. Or when she hears the drowsy plink of a piano key, as she does now in this pub. She does not always find transcendence.

The young woman attends family gatherings. She squeals over the little ones, who, yes, have become *so much bigger* than when she saw them last. She inspects cards, card tables, chairs, and other trappings of relatives.

The young woman meets up with friends here on a somewhat regular basis. While in conversation she drinks after-dinner wine – red, please. She widens her eyes and clasps her hands at appropriate intervals to offer support to these friends. What's more, she senses herself doing this, performing at these sanitised gatherings.

The young woman schedules evening telephone conversations with out of town connections on a somewhat less regular basis. In these conversations, performance may vary. Still, she shall have import on those evenings: she shall have a conversation with an out of town connection.

The young woman reads sometimes. At other times, she turns the pages of publications unseeingly. It matters little what publication is present, only that it *is* present. To her credit, she has tried all manner of material: books on everything from whales to withering glances. The printed page fails to hold the same interest for her as what is unfolding around her when she is reading.

The young woman observes the pub patrons as she finishes up her meal. She gathers energy from observing the interactions of others, glorying in them: one page of her journal notes as much. The world outside pub doors awaits her in due course. While she is in any such establishment – and she *is* in one now, the young woman dutifully reminds herself as she signals for another ale – the world is hers.

In these moments, the young woman wants to counsel, rapturously, 'Go away, go away,' to those who might approach her. She attends to things, imagined and real, dreamily and to the best of her ability. She feels grateful for an awareness of her existence. All is in accord. All will be all right, she feels with certainty.

The young woman schedules her weekends to provide a certain predictability. She often flounces into this pub on a Saturday afternoon. Bright-eyed, her hair loose and stylish, she is full of questions and ideas, schemes, really, for the day and a half that awaits her. On those afternoons her half-supped ale perches precariously at the edge of her table as she takes her journal from her bag and proceeds to work something out in writing. Here, an idea is hotly pursued in a clutch of cramped pages.

After alcoholic consumption, carefully considered, and observation of others around her, the young woman returns to her flat. She collects her grocery list and gets on with the weekly shop. She may drop off a few items at the cleaners; she goes often enough to be able to exchange smiles with regular personnel.

The young woman returns again to her flat, now smelling

of cheese and soap. She cleans herself up and heads for a place of worship, arriving early enough to establish herself near its steps for people-watching. She rotates through a few places in the name of variety, and goes to each often enough to exchange smiles with regulars. But it's not often enough to establish any real rapport with others, or so her conscience admonishes her from time to time.

A few voicemails from friends and, every so often, a young man await the young woman when she returns to her flat following Saturday worship. The friends chirp: *Any interest in meeting up with us?* The young man inquires cautiously: *Any interest in meeting up with me?* The young woman returns the calls apologetically. Sorry, she's booked for the evening.

On these occasions, weather permitting, the young woman slips on her walking shoes and ambles along a popular route, perfect for perusing evening foot traffic. She makes it home as the sky darkens, slipping off her shoes and watching from her window as the sun slips lower. The remaining hours call for music – sometimes contemporary, sometimes classical – and a beverage of some sort and temperature. When the breeze wafts her way, she pours herself a cool glass of wine – red, please – throws on the contemporary jazz, and flings open the windows. When inclement weather necessitates a closed-window approach, she turns to a different beverage (it's not unusual for it to be the remnants of something begun earlier that day at the pub, brought home in her travel mug) unearths a bit of soft classical music from the pile of records, and curls up on the sofa. The room hums with a little night music; she hums and smiles at an evening well spent.

The young woman schedules the end of her weekends to provide a similar predictability. On Sunday afternoons, she is out the door in good time, well rested and dreamy as the world yawns around her. The atmosphere at the pub is different, slower and deliberate, as those around her square their shoulders in anticipation of the coming week. Folk drift in and out. Some are languid, lazy and hazy-eyed from an evening spent listening to music of a different stripe; some tuck in to a roast lunch.

The young woman flits back to her flat, mentally sorting through what she hopes to get from the anticipated week ahead. Is her presentation ready? Is the flat presentable if her friends unexpectedly come to call? Should she accept that invitation to dinner from that male friend-of-sorts? And as long as she's on the subject of food, should she toss out those vegetables, or should she use them in a salad before the week's through?

After leaving the pub on a Sunday, it can come to pass that the young woman does not speak to another person aloud for the rest of the day. The phone rarely rings. The day lacks the orchestral colours of the one before. She prefers this, in her own way. It's a day as she's not had in the six preceding it. What's left of the weekend is hers to pursue, to pursue with industry, and to savour, if she so desires.

To that end, the young woman calls her mother – an exercise in patience for both parties. She cleans the kitchen – in case those friends do come to call. As the weekend wanes, she finds herself with an as yet undigested portion of the newspaper and a new bit of jazz. (It feels almost criminal to toss aside this portion of the paper unread.)

By rights, the young woman should be doing something lovely with such a day: listening to bold music, strolling in a bright gallery with an eye-catching array of goods, halted only by a gentleman discreetly doffing his cap at her. She should be savouring a sweet treat, or perhaps a salty one. (She is pleasantly indecisive in her vision of things.)

The young woman sits here, in this station pub. The comforting coo of conversation calls to her. She sits in the midst of autumn, its colours echoed in the fashions etched around her. She listens to talk on the turning of the seasons and studies the scene. The piano plinks away. She imagines it is pleased to be of use again.

The young woman stands decisively and downs the rest of her ale. She arranges her scarf, squares her shoulders, and sets off into the crowd.

2030

Ticket to Uncanny Valley

by Rose Little

The platform was announced at the last minute and the commuters hurried to get a seat on their homeward train. Jack dodged past a group of 'droids entering the third class carriage and leapt aboard. The whistle blew and the train pulled steadily out of Paddington. As he walked down the swaying aisle he took a good look at the women with an empty seat beside them and chose himself a neat brunette in an open-necked shirt and black skirt, smart jacket hanging on the hook at her side.

'Do you mind if I...?' he began, stopping by her, putting his hand on the back of the empty seat and looking directly at her. He liked to establish eye contact right from the start. The young woman inclined her head just a fraction, then she looked at him properly and her expression seemed to melt a little. He felt triumphant, she was responding to his good looks, his dark hair and blue eyes, his reassuring friendly face.

She smiled. 'Why not?'

This was more encouragement than he'd hoped for. He grinned and slid into the seat beside her. 'On time tonight,' he ventured, the obvious phrase falling from his lips without reflection. *I'll have to do better than that*, he thought, but she replied at once.

'Yes, it's very fast.'

He glanced at her askance, but she looked guilelessly back. She had such lovely brown eyes, all the clichés he had ever read in the 'Rush-Hour Crush' column of his morning *Metro* flowed through his mind: 'Girl with the melting brown eyes', 'I could drown in the depths of your eyes'…

He tore his gaze away though she continued to look at him. Her scrutiny made him uncomfortable, actually, he was not used to such appraisal from a beautiful woman. London was left behind and her face was framed by the golden field behind her, the oilseed rape gleaming in the evening sun as they sped by. She was too perfect, he decided, a peach complexion, the strange eyes expertly outlined in black. Then he caught himself up – could she in fact be *too* perfect, too good to be true? Women nowadays were so clever with their make-up, he couldn't see a single blemish or quirky feature, the flaw that made a face human. She was looking down at her hands now, no doubt checking her perfect nail polish. He must get her attention back.

'You work in the Big Smoke then?' he asked her, but she looked confused so he rephrased: 'Do you work in London?'

She nodded. 'I do general admin.' He wondered at that. The women he picked up usually claimed to be secretaries or PAs at least. 'And you?' she asked in return.

'I work for the *Telegraph*,' he said, hoping she would think he was a journalist. *A cold-calling journalist*, he reflected glumly. But her expression didn't change. Again he had the feeling that she didn't quite follow him. He felt a sudden need to impress her, to make an impact on her impassive face. 'I drive a BMW convertible and live in a penthouse flat,' he told her and laughed to turn it into a joke, if she wanted to take it that way.

He was rewarded with an immediate response. 'Well!' she held out her hand sideways to him and as the train rocked over the points her thigh touched his. 'I'm Zandra!' she said.

He took her hand and her grip was firm. 'Jack,' he replied, his self-assurance returning with the physical contact.

'Are you going a long way?' she asked him.

'Only to Didcot.' He couldn't prevent his voice sounding sulky. He wished he could give a more prestigious address, the harbour at Bristol, say. 'You?'

'Didcot also,' she answered promptly. A coincidence but no reason why she shouldn't be going there too. He risked an immediate follow-up.

'I often stop at the Railway Inn on the way home, do you know it? Do you feel like a drink?'

She looked startled, then nodded her approval. After a pause she asked simply, '"Home"? Are you married?'

Jack managed not to stare at this bald question. 'No, I'm not married,' he replied gravely, for it was a grave business, being married. He found it hard to carry on the conversation for a moment. People getting off at Reading passed them: a woman on her phone; a woman carrying four bags slung about her, one of which bumped his cheek painfully as she passed; a fit and confident-looking man, younger and way cooler than he could ever be, dressed in sports shirt and jeans. A pulse started in Jack's temple when he noticed Zandra's attention drawn to him.

It was impossible to talk above the disembodied *We are arriving into Reading*, and Jack relapsed into a little dream to restore his equilibrium. He had a vision of his flat in Brunel Mansions – he saw Zandra quite clearly reclining on the black leather sofa (such an extravagance) with a drink in her hand, looking at him with those candid brown eyes, surely most unusual in their setting. What lay behind them, what was she thinking? She seemed to be encouraging him as just then she looked up at him through her lashes. It was rare that things happened quite so fast for him. After Reading, as the train gathered speed again on its headlong dash west, he began to move her from his sofa to his bedroom...

The clattering drinks trolley interrupted his happy dream. 'Would you like a cuppa?' he felt bound to ask Zandra. Her eyebrows rose, then relaxed.

'Just a coffee please.'

Jack turned to the service 'droid, glancing up over her square frame to her face out of habit, then quickly dropping his gaze from her fixed and mindless stare.

'Two americanos,' he commanded, and took them without acknowledgement apart from waving his card across her wrist.

The 'droid continued steadily down the carriage, her hydraulics compensating for the train's motion.

As they sipped their coffees Jack couldn't help speculating that it was possible Zandra had been looking for someone the same as he was. She was making no secret of her availability as she crossed her legs in a provocative way. He tried to think of conversation to interest her, he felt sure she would meet him halfway.

'Do you go up to town at the weekend?' he asked her. 'I know a good bar in Soho.'

'I work in Woburn Square,' she offered.

'Do you ever go and see a show?'

'I've not had the opportunity up to now.'

He wondered why not but he didn't want to scare her off by probing further and saying the wrong thing. Plenty of time to talk once he'd got her into the pub.

She startled him with her next question. 'How much do you earn then?' she said. He wondered if she was implying that shows cost a lot of money. Embarrassed, he noticed one or two other passengers seemed to be listening.

'I'll tell you later,' he said, dropping his voice to what he hoped was an intimate note and sketching a wink.

He was relieved when, quite soon after, the train pulled into Didcot and he used the excuse of the pressing crowd to cup her elbow and shepherd her off the train. Surprisingly she took his hand as they walked down the platform to the exit. He squeezed her fingers but she did not respond. What did it matter, he had her to himself now. The Railway Inn was at hand and he almost pushed her through the door.

'What a huge pub!' she exclaimed, looking around. 'Bigger than it looks from the outside.'

Jack laughed. 'You've not been here before? Yes, it's got bedrooms upstairs too.' The background music was rather too loud for talking but he found he wanted to share things with her, it was easier on his home territory. 'It's always been my local. A new company has taken it over recently and they've broken up the space a bit with different zones.' He steered her past a group of people eating at an oval table in the centre. 'I used to come here with my dad when I was a teenager, it was different then.'

There weren't many people in on this Thursday evening as, unusually, there was nothing on. Two or three couples sat closely together and some of the older drinkers sat at the bar. Several young men stood near a pillar with a high ledge running round it which held their pints. They were laughing and talking noisily above the music.

Jack hoped one of the little alcoves at the back would be available, it would be quieter there. It had been different when his dad was around, they used to prop up the bar, then play darts or sit on a squashy old sofa. Now he and Zandra made their way among the mismatched wooden tables, the new owners' idea of bringing things up to date. He chose a former school desk in a booth beside a bookcase. Books were an improvement on the tired old horse brasses, though the books were only decorative, he'd found, in leather bindings with titles in gold, the kind of books nobody ever read. The ancient TV was familiar from his youth, though completely obsolete these days and practically an antique, dating as it did to around the turn of the century.

He waited for her to settle herself, perching on the edge of the banquette and sitting up straight. She didn't have a handbag, just her jacket, which she laid beside her. This was disturbing in some way but he didn't remark on it.

'What will you have?' he asked her. At her bewildered expression he said again, 'What would you like to drink?'

'You choose,' she said, subsiding and smiling submissively up at him. She seemed to look right into his soul. Jack turned away, stumbling slightly, his senses reeling so that he could hardly find his way to the bar.

He came back with two whiskies and sat down across the table from her, where he could look at her. He had a hard job not to keep staring. It was a novelty to have the company of such a lovely girl. There was something about her he couldn't put his finger on, something that fascinated him – besides the obvious. Her breasts were bulging out of her top and the way she was sitting showed them off to advantage. He presumed she was doing it on purpose.

But she was giving away no secrets, she was asking him about his younger self. 'So you've always lived here, and you used to come here with your dad?' She leaned further towards him and seemed genuinely to want to listen to him.

'He was a great dad, he used to spend a lot of time with us, me and my brother.'

'Older or younger brother? It must be good to have siblings.'

'Older. He left when Dad did, got himself a job in Birmingham. He doesn't keep in touch.' He hadn't meant to tell her so much. He didn't want to think about the time after his father had left. And he wasn't quite happy with the way she was taking the initiative, *he* liked to be the one directing the questions, being in control. But she was continuing encouragingly:

'Your father ran away then?'

Jack couldn't help a little laugh in spite of himself at her phrase. 'Not exactly ran away. He told my mother he would have to leave.'

Zandra looked all enquiry, she was so sympathetic. He had never told anyone, but he felt the need to tell *her*.

'He couldn't cope with her gambling habit any longer,' he found himself explaining, though his breath came short. 'I was nearly eighteen so it wasn't so bad.'

She put her hand over his, a gesture of comfort, but it was an electric touch. He began to feel he would have to have her tonight, and felt that he would do anything for her, an eerie feeling he hadn't experienced before. He wasn't sure where he was for the moment and imagined holding her body against his, those soft breasts crushed against him, his mouth descending on hers...

She sipped at her drink and a youth walking past dislodged one of the books from its shelf. It lay where it fell, but like a cog slotting into place it seemed to awaken something in her consciousness.

'Don't you think story books are so sad?' she began.

'Not always.' He thought of the thriller he'd been reading recently. 'They can be entertaining.' *They can be an escape*, he added to himself, but she was pressing on.

'My teacher said sharing our sadness makes us more... human. He did the classics with us, they were all terribly sad: *Jude the Obscure*, *Tess*, even *Middlemarch*.'

He felt on safer ground. 'That's the Victorians. You want to read something from the twenty-first century. What about, *Eleanor Oliphant is Completely Fine?* It's having a come-back since the film: everybody's reading it.' He remembered too late that there was plenty of sadness in that too. He tried again. 'Or why don't you get away from story books and try some non-fiction, what about *Sapiens?*'

But she went on earnestly with her own ideas. 'I think stories should have some moral to them, don't you, and not just entertain us?' She laid a hand on his knee for a moment.

What a compelling woman, an intellectual. He began to suspect things were not what they seemed. She could be a university student, doing a holiday job?

Without waiting for an answer she said suddenly, 'It's scary being a person, isn't it, you don't know how to behave. Each one of us alone in our own heads, how can we know each other?'

This was beyond him, he'd never met anyone like her. 'Do you do a lot of reading?' he brought out at last.

'We had to, in the convent.'

So that was it – the reason for her awkwardness, her odd phraseology and her forwardness (rather welcome), a reaction to her previous lack of freedom. Of course. He began to feel protective towards her, it must be hard facing life in the real world after living in a restrictive order.

'You got your knowledge only from books,' he observed.

She considered. 'Yes, that's true, and I had a good teacher

– tutors came in from the town to teach us, you see. Richard wanted to be able to discuss important things with me, he said: cultural, political, moral things – and history and literature. He made me everything I am. I have tried to model myself on him.' Jack was looking at her, a little awestruck. 'You remind me of him,' she added.

Jack quashed his jealousy of 'Richard' and took this as a compliment. He looked into her face. 'It was brave of you to tell me about the convent, we hardly know each other. People have such prejudices....' He dropped his eyes. He knew he was guilty of this himself.

'I think it's best to be honest. And I am getting to know you. I would like to know you better.' She leant back, resting her arm along the back of the banquette, without breaking eye contact. Her smile, seeming to promise developments, was completely beguiling.

Such frankness. Why did he feel the need to put on a front to this young woman and be other than himself? Jack, with his quite small flat on the third floor and his Ford Escort. A pleasant picture came to him of a relationship where neither of them needed to pretend. *He would tell the truth – then, perhaps, this time....* He glanced up from his drink and met her patient, candid look. She was waiting for him to guide the conversation. He began to see her as a real person for the first time and not just an easy lay. He resolved to find out all about her.

'Did you grow up round here then?' he asked.

'Yes, we had a little house in Manor Road,' she answered.

'Manor Road,' he echoed, impressed. 'You mean one of those half-timbered cottages?'

'Yes,' she replied. 'My parents sent me to Cheltenham Ladies College at first. It was all right. But then I felt drawn to St Mary's at Wantage.'

Jack was tempted to compete with 'Cheltenham Ladies College' though he couldn't manage St Mary's the Virgin. He remembered his newly made resolution, however.

'I went to St Birinus,' he said, referring to the local secondary school. 'I've still got some friends from there.' He paused, recognising that he felt this was a matter for congratulation, though he wasn't sure why. For a moment his continual sense of not being good enough was eased – he was lucky in his friends.

'What is your work?' she asked him in her odd and open way, as he had said no more. There was no limit to her inquisitiveness, and he would have to tell her. She held her whisky glass carelessly and gazed at him. He found her look unnerving.

He thought of his boring yet exacting job selling advertising space, headphones on all day at the communal desk, hardly noticing if it was rain or shine for weeks on end. At the beginning he had meant to try and transfer to the reporting side, but it required more qualifications, more studying than he'd imagined. *Or probably just more networking*, his cynical inner voice muttered.

He took a deep breath to tell her, to lay himself at her feet *– I'm only a junior ad rep, not a journalist, and I feel like a failure* – but at that moment someone Jack recognised as a regular walked in, a retired farmer in a corduroy jacket. His dog was with him as usual, a glossy red setter Jack had often admired and patted.

Strangely, tonight the dog scurried past him, belly to the ground, growling in an uncharacteristic and ugly way. He went straight towards Zandra, his hackles raised. Before Jack or the owner realised what was happening the dog had made a rush at her, snapping at her ankles.

'Hey!' shouted the owner, and ran to grasp the setter's collar, but then, with a brutal kick, Zandra laid the beautiful dog on his back. He lay there squealing in a way dreadful to hear, four paws twitching feebly in the air. The farmer, who had begun to apologise, shouted, 'What the hell!' at Zandra, too shocked to say another word, his attention all for the setter. He picked his dog up in his arms, bending lovingly over him, and carried him quickly out of the door without looking back. There were a few exclamations and some stares, but nobody else had taken in what had actually happened, it had been so fast.

Jack was stupefied, he couldn't bear any cruelty to animals. He managed to say, 'How could you do that?' and looked at Zandra in disbelief, hoping for some kind of explanation. But she only looked back at him and smiled, as if expecting the next round in a game.

As the silence lengthened, Jack began to feel what a fool he'd been. How close he'd come to believing in her, to thinking her a person he could really relate to. Her callousness had repelled him and it struck him that there was something subtly wrong about her, like the negative of a black and white photograph. He no longer found her desirable, she was no kindred spirit after all.

Not caring what she thought of him he mumbled, 'Sorry, got to go,' and strode out of the pub. The door slammed after him.

The old inn had withstood wars and make-overs, quiz nights, music nights, Morris dancers – even the acceptance of unaccompanied women. But it had never seen anything as weird as Zandra.

*

At the bar, the landlord looked up from his newspaper. He hadn't noticed more than the whining dog, and, now it had been removed, the background rumble of the evening drinkers seemed as usual. His wife was still serving cheerfully further up the bar.

He read the headline on page 2: *'Droid Escapes From Lab*, and went on to the subtitle: *Transformative Technology's leading scientist Richard Turner warns latest model has vanished*. Then his eyes fell on the cartoon at the foot of the page depicting an R2D2-type robot rolling away from pursuers. He glanced up as Jack left the pub, abandoning his stunning date. His eyes ran over the woman's body and back to his paper.

Zandra calculated she wouldn't have to sit there on her own for very long. It was true Richard had taught her everything: this was the way humans carried on, using one another for their own ends. Richard had used her for his own entertainment and for the furtherance of his career; Jack, reminding her so much of Richard, had intended to use her too. This time she would be in control. She crossed one elegant leg over the other, looked nonchalantly around the pub, and waited.

About the Authors

Jane Andrews is the author of the *Sarah and Steve* trilogy and the *Dreams and Shadows* fantasy series, both for young adults, and she has published four other novels. Two of her short stories will be published in *Flash* magazine and a Pure Slush anthology later this year.

Sarah Byrne is a writer of fiction for both adults and young adults. By day she is a film and theatre researcher and you can find her talking about all of that on Twitter at @sarahbyrnesays.

Jackie Carpenter has enjoyed words all her life, but only recently started to put them together in short stories and poems. Born in London, she now lives in Derby.

Brenda Cutler: I vowed to grow old disgracefully so I became a member of various groups which gave me the opportunity to attend courses. Courtesy of the U3A and others I have found the time to scribble words down. As a result, writing short stories and anecdotes has become my main hobby.

Sheila Davie has a background in human resources and psychometrics, and enjoys writing light crime stories where there are many twists and turns for the reader to follow.

Mike Evis lives in Abingdon, and has had a lifelong passion for writing, He mainly reads modern literary fiction or science fiction; both genres are reflected in his short stories, of which he has had fourteen published in various anthologies to date (including a novelette length piece of fiction).

Margaret Gallop: I have always loved writing and value my travels and experiences to dip into for ideas. When writing short stories I enjoy entering a world I can barely imagine and attempting to bring it to life.

Alex Fraser was born in Scotland, has worked as a lawyer in London and Oxford and now lives in Wales. He is a writer of short stories as well as non-fiction articles. Alex is currently working on a novel set in a remote Welsh village where a murder forty years ago led to a miscarriage of justice.

Tracy Hewitson: Fifty-something housewife married to Nigel and mother to Georgina. I have a degree in social sciences and was a graduate of the Institute of Personnel and Development. A bit of a dreamer, searching for the soul of humankind.

Tony Lawrence: I am an early-retired businessman, living in North Yorkshire with my wife and our two cats, plus a lodger cat who likes our place better than his owners' house across the road. I am new to writing and also enjoy playing my drums (not very well) as well as booking exotic holidays in the sun to keep my missus happy.

Alice Little: Inspired by literary fiction of the early twentieth century, Alice enjoys writing of all kinds. She has had seventeen short stories published since 2016, as well as releasing four collections of her work. Find out more at alicelittle.co.uk/fiction and follow her on Twitter and Instagram at @littleamiss.

Rose Little: Taking a step back from 'real' life and making up a story has always appealed to me and I started writing when very young. The short story is my favourite genre, although I am currently working on a series of linked stories based on my experiences teaching in Kenya some time ago. The support and fun of belonging to Didcot Writers has proved invaluable.

Ian Marshall: Originally from East Sussex, Ian now resides in the wild-west province of Alberta. It is here he can be found referring to himself in the third person while trying to evade the dangerous clutches of moose, bears and the Royal Canadian Mounted Police.

Eugenie Pusenjak: I grew up in Perth, Western Australia, and now live in Canberra with my partner Craig. By day, I'm an in-house lawyer for a government department. In my spare time, I'm a writer, reader, baker, gardener, trivia nerd, and Whovian. This story was inspired by the documentary *Churchill's Secret Army*.

Vanessa Waltz has published work with the Anne Frank House in Amsterdam, *The Fortnightly Review* in France, *Mslexia* in Newcastle, and *Trollopiana* in Tunbridge Wells. She holds an MA in English from Middlebury College in the United States and completed her studies at Lincoln College, Oxford.

Grant Waters is a portrait painter based in Oxfordshire. When not painting he is a college lecturer. He has been spinning yarns for his children at bedtime for a good few years and has latterly tried his hand at writing more adult fare.

Other Books

First Contact
This anthology was published in September 2019, and features thirty-one stories from thirty authors from Didcot and beyond, in a range of genres and styles. From meeting a stranger in 1970s Africa to adopting a child, from a mass hallucination to making contact with criminals – this book considers first encounters and new beginnings – and what happens next.

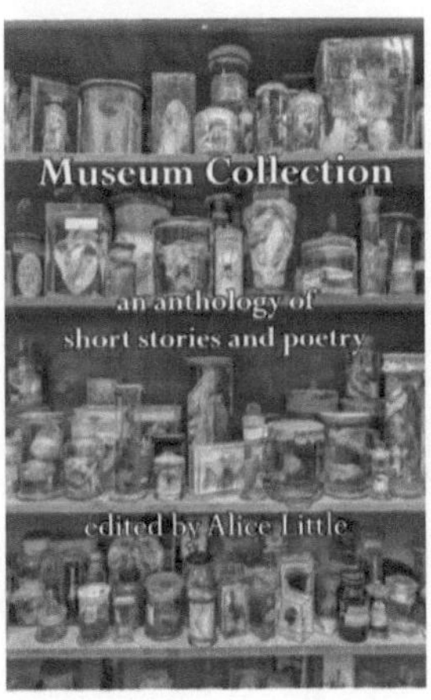

Museum Collection: an anthology of short stories and poetry
This accumulation of acquisitions, this cabinet of curiosities, this Museum Collection brings together a selection of short stories and poetry inspired by museums, galleries, art and artefacts. From artifice to archaeology, from exhibition halls to archives – and spanning genres from thriller to comedy – why not take a look at what's on display?

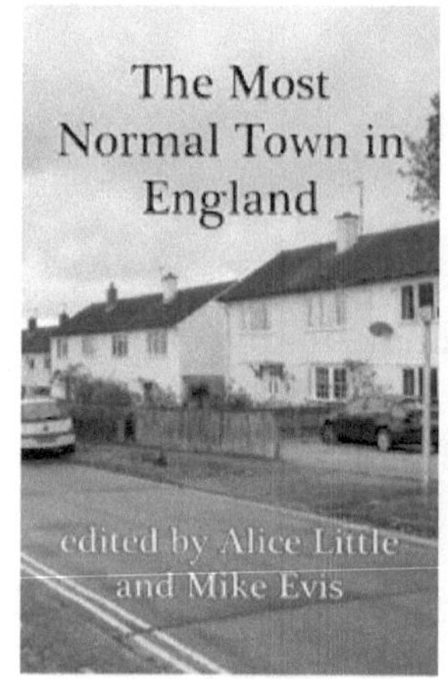

The Most Normal Town in England
In this anthology authors were challenged to consider what makes a town normal – or not: who lives there, who never leaves, what skeletons are lurking in the closets? From sci-fi to romance, from horror to literary fiction, this book contains 42 stories by 40 authors detailing the happenings in a range of apparently normal English towns, villages and cities.

Compositions: a collection of short stories on the theme of music
The stories in this book were selected from among the submissions to Didcot Writers' summer competition 2018. You can read some of the stories online at didcotwriters.wordpress.com, where you can also find out about new opportunities.

From musicians to collectors, instruments to electronics, this book approaches the theme of music from a range of directions.